P9-ASB-323

WHAT VENGEANCE COMES

A John Decker Thriller

ANTHONY M. STRONG

Also by Anthony M. Strong

The John Decker Thriller Series

What Vengeance Comes

Cold Sanctuary

Crimson Deep

Grendel's Labyrinth

Whitechapel Rising

Black Tide

Ghost Canyon

John Decker Series Prequel

Soul Catcher

The Remnants Series

The Remnants of Yesterday

Standalone Books

The Haunting of Willow House

Crow Song

For a complete list of books by the author, visit AnthonyMStrong.com

West Street Publishing

This is a work of fiction. Characters, names, places, and events are products of the author's imagination. Any similarity to events or places, or real persons, living or dead, is purely coincidental.

Copyright © 2020 by Anthony M. Strong
All rights reserved.

No part of this book may be reproduced in any form or by any electronic or mechanical means, including information storage and retrieval systems, without written permission from the author, except for the use of brief quotations in a book review.

Cover art and interior design by Bad Dog Media, LLC.

ISBN: 978-1942207030

For Sonya - who scares easily

A word from the author.

The Loup-Garou, sometimes referred to as a Rougarou, is an old Cajun French werewolf legend. Often used as a method of gaining obedience, the wolf-like beast may hunt down Catholics who don't follow the rules of Lent, or might come for misbehaving children.

Other variations of the myth describe a person who changes into the Loup-Garou for 101 days, able to switch between their human form and beast. Unlike other werewolf myths, the beast is not directly affected by the full moon.

In Cajun legend the Loup-Garou roams the forests and swamps of Louisiana around New Orleans, as a product of witchcraft, with either the witch herself turning into the monster, or cursing others to become the beast.

Prologue

32 Years Ago

THE WAITING ROOM was cold and clinical. An odor of disinfectant clung to the air, cloying and pungent. Concealed fluorescent lighting, set into the ceiling behind yellowed plastic grilles, bounced a cool white glow from the dull gray walls, giving the appearance that the whole room was overexposed, making everything appear painfully bright.

A row of hard plastic chairs lined the wall, empty except for one, upon which perched a ten-year-old boy, his curly black hair cropped short, a small bruise over his left cheek where a badly thrown baseball made contact two Saturdays before. He rocked back and forth on the edge of the seat, nervous and fidgeting.

Voices, low and muted, drifted through a set of white double doors. The boy did not know what the occupants of the room beyond the doors were saying. Despite his attempts to listen in, he could not hear them clearly, but he knew it was not good. Nothing had been good for days.

A tear pushed from the corner of the boy's eye and meandered down his cheek. He wiped it away before standing up, then counted out the steps to the double doors, looking down at the ground to make sure his feet remained within the confines of the light blue tiles as he walked, careful not to let them land in-between, over the grout lines. Todd Jenkins two houses down had told him it was bad luck to step on the lines between the tiles, and he needed no more of that, not right now.

When he reached the doors, he put a hand out and pushed them open just wide enough to glimpse what lay beyond, but could not make sense of anything. He eased them wider, careful not to make a sound, until the room came into view, and what he saw froze him to the spot.

His mother lay on a hard aluminum table. A strange circular light hovered like a weird alien spaceship above her. He knew it was his mother because an arm had slipped down and now dangled, fingers pointing toward the floor. Upon that arm, near her wrist, was a heart-shaped tattoo with a set of initials inked into it - his father's initials. He'd heard the story of that tattoo so many times he knew it as well as he knew his own name. She'd gotten it a few weeks after she met his father, to prove her love on a whim. The tattoo left no doubt who occupied the table, even though her body was covered with a white sheet, the fabric stained crimson in places like a grotesque Rorschach test.

He stood transfixed, horrified yet unable to move. The men in the room were still talking, but then, as if sensing the pair of childish eyes invading the forbidden space, one of them turned, a look of deep sadness upon his face.

"You shouldn't be here, Johnny boy," his father said, crossing the gap between them. "You need to stay in the waiting room. I'll be out very soon, I promise."

John eyed him, relieved that his view of the mortuary table was blocked, that he was unable to see the nightmare that lay upon it, the bloody thing that was once his mother. Instead, he saw his father, stiff and weary, his sheriff uniform uncharacteristically wrinkled. And he saw the gun in its leather holster, right there, just waiting.

For a moment John wondered if he could snatch it and turn it upon himself, pull the trigger and join his mother in heaven, which was surely where she was. He ached to see her again. But Father Gregory, his Sunday school teacher, said suicide was a mortal sin, and sinners went to hell, not heaven, so it would be a pointless endeavor.

It was too late now, anyway. His father was steering him backward, closing the double doors, locking them.

John turned away, hands deep in his pockets, and started to weep, ever so softly.

Chapter 1

Present Day - Wolf Haven, Louisiana

SHERIFF JOHN DECKER steered the police cruiser along the winding, muddy trail toward the cabin in the woods.

In the passenger seat Beau Thornton, Mayor of the town of Wolf Haven, leafed through a pile of paperwork resting on his lap.

"I sure do appreciate you bringing me out here at such short notice, Sheriff," he said in a thick southern accent, never once looking up from the stack of papers. "I know you have a lot on your plate."

"Don't mention it," Decker replied. He might be elected, just like Beau, but Thornton still cut his paychecks. "I'm not sure why you need me though."

"I thought it would be prudent to have a show of force on hand when I speak to Annie."

Decker shot him a sideways glance and raised an eyebrow.

"Alright, you got me." The mayor threw his arms up. "The damn woman gives me the creeps. Living out here in the middle of nowhere surrounded by alligators and mosquitos. People say she's a witch you know."

"You really believe that?" Decker knew the stories, just like everyone else who had grown up in Wolf Haven. The town kids had been calling Annie Doucet a witch since he was a boy, probably even before that. It was just nonsense, but the Cajuns took their superstitions seriously in these parts. "Just because she's a little odd–"

"A little odd? Don't make me laugh," Mayor Thornton guffawed. "She's certifiably crazy is what she is."

"That still doesn't make her a witch." Decker swung the car off the track and pulled up in front of the cabin. "Here we are then."

"You're coming in with me, right?"

"Of course. Wouldn't want you to face an old woman all on your own." Decker opened his door and waited while his passenger climbed out of the cruiser. If the Mayor caught the sarcasm in the sheriff's voice he didn't show it.

They were about to climb the three worn wooden steps leading up to the cabin when the front door swung silently inward.

"Looks like she's expecting us," Decker said. "Almost like she saw us coming in her crystal ball."

"Not funny," Beau responded as a frail shape emerged from the cabin.

Annie Doucet stood in the doorway, observing them with black beady eyes. "Wondered when you'd show up Beau Thornton."

"Well hello there Annie," the mayor replied, his face stoic.

"I see you brought your lapdog sheriff along for the ride."

"Now don't be like that Annie."

"I'll do as I will." Annie turned and retreated back through the door. "You'd better come on in and say your piece, time's wasting."

Chapter 2

THE INTERIOR of the cabin smelled like old socks and mold. A kerosene lamp hung from a beam above their heads, the flame doing little to illuminate the dank one-room hut. "Good god, she doesn't even have electric service," Thornton whispered, covering his mouth with his hand as if that would somehow shield the fact that he was speaking. "What a way to live."

"Shut up or she'll never agree to sell you her land." Decker cast his eyes around, picking out sticks of furniture in the gloom. A rocking chair occupied one corner, while a metal frame bed took up the other. In the center of the hut stood a table and two chairs. The only other thing in the cabin was a wood-burning stove with a belly that glowed red despite the humid weather outside.

Thornton turned to the old woman. "I have some documents for you to sign." He held the sheaf of papers out. His hand shook a little. "Then we can put this nasty business behind us and move on."

"What if I don't want to sign?" Annie peered at them with hooded eyes set into bony sockets. "This land has been in my family for six generations."

"I appreciate that Annie, I do, but this here is progress. The town needs that road out to the Interstate. Your land is slap bang in the middle of the route."

"Not my problem."

"See, that's where you're wrong," Thornton said. "If you don't sign these papers, take the money we're offering you, then the State will purchase the land against your will."

"The answer's still no." Annie didn't raise her voice, but neither Decker nor Thornton could fail to miss the anger behind the words. "You take your papers, and your check, back where you got them."

"I'm going to leave these here." Thornton deposited the paperwork on the table and backed up. "Take a few days to look over them. You'll see we're making you a very generous offer considering your land is nothing but mosquito infested swamp."

"You'll regret this." Annie's voice was dry, rasping.

"I doubt it." Thornton turned toward the door. "Come along sheriff. Why don't you drive me back to town."

Decker followed the mayor back into the sunlight, relieved to be away from the gloom inside the cabin. He wished he hadn't agreed to escort the mayor up here. It seemed wrong to be forcing this frail old woman out of her home just so that they could build a road. But at the end of the day it wasn't his call.

ANNIE DOUCET WATCHED the two men depart. She waited until the police cruiser was out of sight before turning back to the interior of the cabin, then scooped up the papers and threw them into the wood-burning stove. She watched the flames lick hungrily at the documents, reducing them to ash.

Walking to a shelf packed with old books, she selected a volume and laid it out on the table, leafing through dry brown pages as frail as she was. She paused at a page toward the middle of the book and stooped low to make out the text, running a bony finger along the paper, tracing the hand-written words as she read them.

Next, the old woman shuffled to her bed. She bent and dragged a chest out from underneath. She opened it and pulled out several mason jars, selecting each for the contents within, and a small copper bowl.

She brought the jars and bowl to the table and mixed the ingredients, careful to follow the instructions in the book, humming a tune to herself as she did so.

It wouldn't be long now, and then she would show the good folk of Wolf Haven just what she thought of their road…

Chapter 3

FLOYD BENSON LIFTED another jug into the flatbed and winced as a stab of pain shot up his back. He was getting too old for this kind of thing.

"Get a move on in there, Terry." He called, glancing toward the makeshift toilet which was, in reality, nothing more than a depression in the ground surrounded by stained tarpaulins. "Did you fall down the hole?"

"I'll be out in a second." Terry Boudreaux's voice drifted from the latrine. "That's the last time I order the Red Beans and Rice at Cassidy's. Damn stuff went and gave me the shits."

"Too much information, Terry." Floyd doubted it was the Red Beans and Rice. He'd eaten the same thing, and he was just fine. It was more likely to be the days old Gumbo he'd brought with him and consumed cold on the drive to the camp. He doubted if Terry bothered to refrigerate it either. The boy was dumber than a box of rocks.

He lifted another jug, the liquid inside shifting when he heaved it toward the truck. He dropped it down on the bed with a grunt and counted his work. Sixteen containers loaded and ready to go. Not bad.

There was still no sign of Terry. If he didn't get a move on they would be late for the drop, and that would not be good, not good at all. "Come on, boy, for Chrissakes. This moonshine ain't gonna drive itself."

The flaps of the latrine parted and Terry emerged, a scowl plastered across his face. "Alright, alright. I'm coming. Quit your bellyaching."

"You want a payday or not?" Floyd wished he could ditch Terry, find someone with a little more ambition, but he couldn't. The boy was his nephew, and like they said, you can't pick your family.

"Where are we going tonight anyhow?" Terry approached the truck cab and hopped into the driver's seat, pulling the door closed.

"Bellows Creek."

"Shit, that's miles away. We won't get back before dawn."

"So? You got a hot date or something?"

"Maybe I do."

"Yeah, right. Don't make me laugh." Floyd chuckled as he took his place in the passenger seat next to his nephew. "Well, what are you waiting for? Let's go."

Terry put the truck in gear and coaxed the vehicle forward. He reached out and snapped on the headlights, their twin beams illuminating the patch of open ground nestled between the tall pine trees, the gin still nestled under a green tarp strung between the tree trunks, and the rows of empty jugs waiting to be filled with liquor.

"Shut those lights off you damn fool," Floyd said, shooting Terry a sharp look. "You'll have every cop in the parish down on us."

"Alright. Sorry." Terry killed the lights. "So how am I supposed to see where I'm going?"

"It's a full moon you dipshit. There's plenty of light." Floyd exclaimed. "Just take it slow and easy."

"Yeah, right. Just don't blame me if we run into a tree."

Terry inched the truck forward until he was out of the clearing, then picked up a little speed when he reached the dirt track. He hunched over the wheel, concentrating as he steered the vehicle down the center of the trail.

They drove in silence for the next five miles. It was only when they reached the paved road and the lights of Wolf Haven appeared on the horizon that Floyd spoke again. "Take Route 16. It'll skirt the town."

"That'll take us miles out of our way," Terry protested. "River Road is quicker."

"And it goes right through the center of Wolf Haven."

"So what? It's 2am, who's gonna see us?"

"Sheriff Decker for one. You think he's tucked up in bed right now with a cup of cocoa and a good book?" If Floyd knew the full moon was the best time to move moonshine, then so did the sheriff. "Just do what I say."

"Fine, but it's not my fault if we're late."

"Hell, yes it is. If you'd helped me load the truck instead of spending the whole damn time taking a crap we'd have been on the road half an hour ago."

"Whatever you say." Terry lapsed into a sullen silence.

Floyd settled back into the seat and looked out at the pinewoods, watching the trees slip by as they made their way toward town. When they reached a fork in the road Terry turned right, onto Route 16. They picked their way through the woods. Terry drove slower than Floyd would have liked, taking the curves at a painful pace, but complaining did no good. The boy didn't know what a gas pedal was.

He closed his eyes and yawned, overcome by a deep weariness. That was the problem with this business, you had to do everything after dark, and Floyd was not a night owl. He found it almost impossible to sleep when the sun was up. He wondered why he'd ever gotten into running moonshine in the first place. Back then, in the mid-sixties, things had been different. The cops were easier to bribe, and the Alcohol and

Tobacco agents didn't have all the fancy gizmos they used today, like thermal imaging cameras and helicopters. Thank god he had a get out of jail free card in the form of a nice fat check from the state, courtesy of Mayor Thornton and the local Chamber. A year from now his land would have a few miles of blacktop running through it, and he would be living high off the proceeds somewhere far, far away.

"Shit."

A jolting lurch rocked Floyd from his slumber. Terry slammed on the brakes hard, bringing the car to a halt in the middle of the road. "What in the hell are you doing now, boy?"

"Holy shit on a shovel. Did you see that?"

"See what?" Floyd peered through the dirt-streaked windshield, but all he saw was the empty road slicing through the pine trees, and beyond that nothing but murky blackness.

"There was something standing there, in the middle of the road," Terry gulped. "It looked right at me."

"We're in the woods genius. It was probably a possum."

"You think I can't recognize a possum when I see it?" Terry flicked on the headlights and leaned forward, his eyes scanning the road. "Besides, it was too big for that, it was more like a man, bigger maybe."

"A bear then. I don't know."

"When was the last time you saw a bear in these parts?"

"What else could it be?" Floyd settled down into the seat. He was growing tired of the conversation. There was clearly nothing in their way, and he wanted to get back to the business of delivering moonshine. Besides, they stuck out like a sore thumb sitting there with the engine idling and their headlamps lighting the place up like it was Christmas.

"I know what I saw."

"Well, there's nothing there now." Floyd pulled a packet of cigarettes from his shirt pocket. "Let's get a move on." He opened the pack, pulled one out, and lifted it to his lips. He was about to light it when a mighty crash rocked the truck. The cigarette fell from Floyd's lips and disappeared between his legs into the seat well.

"Shit. What the hell was that?" Terry's eyes flew wide.

"How would I know?" Floyd opened the glove box and pulled out a .22 revolver as a second crash split the night. The truck shook. "It sounded like it came from the back. Go take a look."

"Me? You go look. You're the one with the gun."

"You're half my age." Floyd held the weapon out. "Here, take it."

"Is it loaded?"

"Well, what good would it be if it wasn't?"

"Just asking." Terry took the revolver and weighed it in his hand. He pulled on the door handle and swung the truck door open. He hesitated.

"What now?" Floyd said. "Don't tell me you're too chickenshit."

"Maybe we should go together."

"Just get out there." Floyd leaned over and gave the younger man a push. "And be careful with that gun. Try not to shoot yourself."

Terry grumbled and climbed from the truck, disappearing into the black void behind the vehicle.

"You see anything?" Floyd adjusted the rear-view mirror but all he saw was darkness.

"Not yet. Hold on." Terry's voice drifted back toward him. There was a moment of silence, and then he spoke again. "Dammit Floyd. Did you shut the tailgate before we left?"

"Course I did. What kind of stupid question is that?" Floyd hollered back. "What's going on?"

"We have a problem." Terry's voice sounded distant. "You'd better get back here."

"This had better be good." Floyd kicked his door open and climbed from the cab, his legs protesting the work. He reached the back of the truck and stopped, his jaw falling open in surprise.

"Son of a bitch." He turned and kicked the rear fender of the truck, ignoring the pain that shot up his leg. "Shit."

Sixteen jugs of moonshine lay shattered on the tarmac, the valuable liquid spreading across the blacktop and running onto the dirt at the road's edge where it soaked into the thirsty soil. His companion was nowhere in sight.

"Terry?" Floyd hollered. "What are you playing at boy?"

All he got was silence in return. A prickle of fear edged its way up his spine.

"Terry, you out here?" He whispered the words, not sure why he was bothering to keep his voice down.

Still nothing.

He turned, looking in both directions, examining the woods, the gaps between the trees, for any sign of the younger man. Terry was nowhere to be found.

"Come on son, this ain't funny no more." If this was Terry's idea of a joke Floyd would kick the boy's ass, half his age or not.

The moon slipped behind the clouds blanketing the road in darkness. Floyd backed up, stopping when he felt the tailgate of the truck push against his back.

"Terry?" He whispered into the blackness.

The clouds scudded across the sky, releasing the moon from their grip, and illuminated the road once again.

"Screw this." Floyd muttered, turning back toward the truck. He did not want to be out here anymore. He'd always had a sixth sense when things weren't right, it was what kept him one step ahead of the law, and this was about as far from right as it got.

"Floyd?" A voice carried on the wind.

Floyd froze. "Terry, that you, boy?"

"Help."

"Where you at boy?" Floyd kept his voice low.

"Please, help me."

Floyd followed the voice. It seemed to be coming from his left, beyond the tree line.

"Hold on Terry, I'm on my way." He picked his way forward, toward the voice, pushing through the undergrowth as he stepped from the road.

"Hurry." Terry sounded desperate.

Floyd picked up the pace, pushing branches aside as he penetrated deeper into the hardwoods, avoiding the trunks of tall pine trees as they loomed out of the darkness.

It didn't take him long to find Terry. The younger man was propped up against a Hickory tree, his legs splayed out at an unnatural angle. The grimace of pain on his face sent a shudder through Floyd.

"You alright there Terry?" Floyd asked, despite the evidence to the contrary. He edged closer.

"It hurts." Terry's voice seemed weak, rasping. "I think my legs are broken."

"Who did this to you?" Floyd noticed that Terry no longer had the gun. He wondered where it was. He would sure feel safer with the weapon in his hands.

"Oh God, it's coming back." Terry's eyes were wide with pain and fear. His voice raised an octave, shrill and thin. "It's coming back for me. Oh no. No, no, no."

"Who's coming boy?" Floyd asked. "Who did this to you?" He'd heard that some other moonshiners were resorting to more extreme measures to knock their rivals out of business. Times were tough. Fewer people wanted illegal hooch these days, but to resort to this?

"Get me out of here."

"But your legs…" One glance told Floyd that Terry couldn't walk. "It's gonna hurt like hell."

"I don't care. For pity's sake." The look on Terry's face convinced Floyd that they should leave, and sooner rather than later.

He took a step forward.

A sharp crack resounded through the forest.

Floyd spun around, searching for the source of the sound.

A branch snapped, closer this time.

"Oh god, not again." Terry shrieked. He tried to stand but his legs buckled under him. He let out a cry of pain and sank back to the ground.

A growl rose on the night air, deep and guttural. A chilling sound that made Floyd's blood run cold.

Instinct took over. He turned and ran, all thought of helping his nephew abandoned. He plummeted headlong through the woods, back toward the road, moving faster than he had in over two decades.

Something crashed along in pursuit, something big and snarling, and it was getting closer.

Just as he thought he would make it, just when he could see the road through the trees, it caught up.

Strong hands gripped him, lifted him high. Curved claws, wicked and sharp, buried themselves into his shoulders like daggers. He sensed hot, rancid breath on his neck, and then he felt the teeth...

Chapter 4

AT NINE-FIFTEEN THE next morning Sheriff John Decker drove his cruiser down Main Street in the direction of Cassidy's Diner, where a steaming hot cup of coffee waited with his name on it. To his right he passed the town library, which occupied a white colonial-style house dating back to 1806, while on his left was the park, complete with the gazebo that the local chamber of commerce had erected a few years before. The gazebo was supposed to revitalize the main drag. There were going to be monthly concerts, weather permitting, every third Saturday afternoon. But all the Chamber had managed were two events thus far. The fact that the town of Wolf Haven, population one thousand seven hundred and thirty, only had one live band didn't help. The fact that the combined age of the three members of that band was over two centuries also didn't help.

Still, that wasn't the only thing the Chamber had done. The new spur off the Interstate would bring much-needed business to the town. He had to hand it to them. They had done a pretty good job of lobbying the Parish and State for the road. No mean feat for a handful of locals who all ran their own businesses too. On the day the project received the green light the Mayor held a party, strutting around puffing his chest out as though he were the architect of the entire thing. Which he was not.

Still, not everyone was happy about the road. To put it in, they needed land, and when the state surveyor came up with a route, it meant buying up several tracts north of town, a few of which were owned by residents not too eager to sell. Most had come around. Except one. The old woman everyone called a witch, Annie Doucet. She seemed hell bent on keeping her land despite the best efforts of everyone from the Mayor to the County Clerk. He hoped she would come around. If she didn't, they would take her land anyway, eminent domain, and he could just guess who they would expect to enforce that.

He reached Cassidy's Diner and eased the squad car in between a pickup truck and a red Toyota Camry that belonged to Taylor Cassidy, daughter of the owner.

He was barely out of the car when he heard a familiar voice boom a greeting.

"Howdy, Decker."

"That's Sheriff Decker if you don't mind." He turned to see Ed Johnson, owner of the County Line Saloon, walking toward him, a donut grasped in his hand. "You're up early today."

"Tell me about it." He grumbled. "The walk-in is on the fritz again."

"Sorry to hear that."

"Me too." Ed pushed half the donut into his mouth and bit down, talking as he chewed. "Repair guy said he would be over by ten to fix it." Crumbs of fried dough fell from between his lips and onto his shirt. He brushed them away.

"Well, good luck." Decker said.

"Thanks." Ed took off in the saloon's direction, a block down the street, pulling a set of keys from his pocket as he went.

Decker turned toward the diner and pulled the door open. A bell rang when he entered.

Nancy Cassidy, the namesake owner of the place, greeted him from behind the counter.

"Morning, Sheriff. You're looking cheerful today." Nancy Cassidy had been one of the major forces behind the new road, and as owner of the only real eating establishment in town and once the spur was built she stood to see a nice rise in business.

"I will be when I've gotten a cup of your steaming hot coffee inside of me." Decker took a moment to admire Nancy. The way her auburn hair fell over her shoulders, her tapered waist that looked good even in an old apron. She might be pushing forty, but she looked easily ten years younger. For a moment he was back in high school. It was their senior year, and he was taking her to the prom. He could still remember how she looked in her dress, coming down the stairs that night. Even now twenty-two years later the memory still could take his breath away.

"You having breakfast too?" she asked in her southern Cajun drawl. "The Crawfish Scrambled Eggs are to die for."

"Not today, Nancy." Decker looked around, his eyes roaming the familiar diner. The place hadn't changed since he was a kid. Chrome and leather stools lined the counter. The tables featured personal jukeboxes that had not worked for at least a decade. Nancy said she kept them because they reminded her of the place when her parents owned it. The restaurant was empty, all except for the booth furthest from the door. This was occupied by Taylor, Nancy's daughter. She ignored them, tapping away on her cell phone in a world of her own. Decker turned his attention back to the counter. "Looks like a slow one."

"It's Saturday morning. Everyone's in bed sleeping off last night or catching a few extra weekend winks. They'll come on by when they get hungry."

Decker watched Nancy pour a tall mug of coffee and set it down in front of him. "How much do I owe you?"

"On the house."

"Now, Nancy, you can't keep giving stuff away like this."

"I know, I know. But the way I see it, you're keeping the streets of Wolf Haven safe for folk to come out and eat here. Besides, I kinda like you." She flashed him a shy smile.

"Well, I like you too, Nancy." He thought he detected the faintest trace of a blush redden her cheeks. "But if you go out of business I won't have anywhere to get my cup of coffee in the morning now will I?" Decker slid four dollars across the counter. "Besides, the worst thing that's happened to this town in the last twelve months was a cat stuck up a tree at the old Gibbs place. It's not like we need much protecting."

"Long may it last," Nancy pulled the tops from the sugar containers on the counter and refilled them one by one.

"Amen to that." Sheriff Decker agreed. Sometimes he still found it odd that he was back here. When he'd left for college he swore never to return to Wolf Haven, but things change. People change. Still, the one good thing about coming back was Nancy. He'd always felt there was unresolved business between them. He knew how much it hurt her when he left. Maybe he should have taken her with him… But that wasn't what happened, and he could not change the past.

He could get a refill of coffee though.

He was about to slide his mug across the counter when his radio squawked. It looked like he wouldn't get a second coffee. Not this morning.

Chapter 5

TAYLOR CASSIDY WATCHED the sheriff flirt with her mother. It made her want to throw up. He was ancient. A dinosaur. Not that her mother was any spring chicken herself. She'd be thirty-nine in a month's time. It didn't bear thinking about.

Taylor turned her attention back to the phone, to her conversation with Jake.

'What are you up to?' The words appeared in a gray bubble.

'Nothing much,' she typed back, watching the screen update with her own blue text box. 'The sheriff is here hitting on my mom.'

'Yuck.'

'I know. Gross.'

'Maybe they'll get together and then he will be your dad.'

'Ew. Don't even go there.' She glanced up. The sheriff was watching her mother, his eyes following her as she went about her business behind the counter.

Her phone buzzed. She looked back down, at the new message that had appeared.

'You want to do something later?'

'Maybe. Do you have anything in mind?' She typed quickly, her fingers dancing over the on screen keyboard.

'We could catch a movie.'

'IDK.' She hit send.

'Bowling?'

'Really?' She stifled a snort. Like she wanted to spend the afternoon in a moldy old bowling alley watching Jake and his buddies roll spares and do high fives.

'What then?'

'Sullivan's Pond.' She glanced back toward the counter. Her mother was there, but Sheriff Decker was gone. When she looked through the plate-glass window fronting the street, she noticed that the parking spot his cruiser had occupied was empty now. Good. He wasn't coming back.

'When?' The phone buzzed.

She read the message and tapped out an answer. 'Pick me up at eleven. I'll wait outside.'

'OK.'

'Bring a towel.' This was fantastic. She hadn't been to the swimming hole since last summer. It was a gorgeous day outside. The temperature was slated to hit ninety. She put the phone down and settled back into the booth with a grin on her face. This was going to be so much fun.

Chapter 6

BY THE TIME Decker arrived at the abandoned truck out on Route 16 Chad Hardwick, his deputy, had already set up warning flares on each side of the pickup and was busy rooting through the glove box, looking for the registration.

When he heard Decker approach, he extracted himself from the cab. "This is a pretty mess we have ourselves here." He wiped his hands on his trousers then inspected his palms as if he expected to see something untoward there. Finally he looked back up at Decker. "There's no registration in the glove box. Although there is an empty gun holster."

"I don't need a registration." Decker said, eyeing the pickup. "I recognize this truck. It belongs to Floyd Benson."

"The moonshiner?"

"The same."

"Well, that would explain some things," Chad said, his eyes straying to the road. "Look over there."

Decker followed the deputy's gaze. Strewn across the blacktop behind the pickup was a mess of smashed jugs. Broken glass glinted in the sunlight. The stench of alcohol lingered even though most of the liquid had already evaporated. "Looks like Floyd lost his load of hooch."

"Seems odd that he'd leave the evidence laying out here in plain sight." Chad leaned against the truck bed and adjusted his hat to shield his eyes from the glare.

"Little bit."

"So where is the old bastard?"

"Maybe he broke down. He has a few acres of land near to here. He could have hiked back up the road."

"And left his truck running? The keys are still in the ignition and the gas tank is empty. Besides, there must have been two people in the truck. Both doors were open when I arrived on scene."

Decker leaned into the cab, noticing the headlight switch. "He left his lights on, too." He turned the radio knob, but nothing happened. "Battery's dead."

"So we've got an abandoned truck with a dead battery and no gas. Smashed alcohol containers all over the road..."

"And no sign of the vehicle's occupants." Decker finished the sentence.

"Let's not forget the empty holster. Presumably there used to be a gun in it," Chad surmised.

"That too."

"Do you think the bottles were smashed before or after he abandoned the truck?" Chad asked.

"Floyd would never leave his hooch unguarded. He was here when this happened. Question is, what made him stop in the first place?"

"Rival moonshiners cutting down on the competition?" Chad speculated. "Maybe he had no choice."

"Maybe. It would explain the smashed jugs and the missing gun. A man like Floyd would not take kindly to being waylaid."

"So where is he then?"

"Good question." Decker said, his gaze roaming back to the truck. "Do you have your camera in the car?"

"Sure do."

Decker nodded. "We should document the scene. I'm not sure if any crime has been committed, except for the obvious one, the illegal transportation of liquor, but we'd better collect evidence anyhow."

"Right you are." Chad sprinted past the pickup truck and leaned inside his police cruiser. He came back a moment later with a digital camera. He slipped the lens cap off and circled the vehicle, reeling off several photographs of the broken liquor bottles, adjusting the lens to take close ups here and there. Next he turned his attention to the bed of the truck. He lifted the camera to his eye, about to snap another picture, when he stopped. "Boss? You should see this."

Decker rounded the back of the truck and looked inside. The bed was empty. "What am I looking at?"

"Right here." Chad reached down, slinging the camera over his shoulder as he did so. "Look at this."

Decker looked to where Chad was pointing and saw it. Stuck into the hard black plastic of the bed liner was a curved white object. "Well now, that shouldn't be there."

Chad focused the camera and fired off three images in rapid succession. "What do you think it is?"

"No idea." Decker pulled a napkin from his pocket and grasped the object between thumb and forefinger. Her worked it free and lifted it out.

"Well?" Chad asked. "What is it?"

"A claw." Decker spoke the words slowly, his attention focused on the talon held between his fingers. "A really big, mean-looking claw."

Chapter 7

TAYLOR HURRIED FROM THE DINER, her phone clutched in her hand, eager to see Jake. A tingle of excitement fluttered in her stomach at the thought of spending the afternoon with him. They had only been dating for six weeks, but somehow she knew he was the one.

This is going to be great, she thought, as she hurried along the sidewalk, looking for his beat up junker of a car. It amused her that he was so proud of it, despite how often it wouldn't start, especially on cold days. The car leaked oil like a sieve, burned through a gallon of gas every five miles, and the trunk didn't lock. The thing had already left a large viscous black stain on the driveway that ran past the diner to their house at the rear. Her mother was not pleased about that, but Taylor didn't care. So what if he drove a moving money pit? He'd earned every penny he spent on that car. That was why she let him drive most of the time, although her own vehicle was miles ahead in comfort and reliability, not to mention more economical. The only exception she made was if they were going to make out. Then she insisted on driving the Camry. It was smaller, and afforded them less room to fool around, but the seats were softer and there was no chance a spring was going to stick you in the butt just when things were getting interesting. Not that she ever allowed things to get too interesting, at least not yet. The way she was feeling recently about Jake though, who knew...

Taylor glanced down at her phone. She started to tap out a message telling Jake to hurry up. That was when she walked headlong into the old woman.

Taylor looked up, startled.

She recognized Annie Doucet instantly.

A tight knot formed in her throat.

"Sorry," she croaked, her voice refusing to cooperate.

The old woman fixed her with an icy stare but said nothing. The corner of her mouth twitched. A strand of wiry gray hair blew across her forehead.

"I really am sorry," Taylor repeated, remembering the childhood stories that Annie was a witch. That she ate toads caught in the swamps and cast spells under the full moon. They said she could put a hex on a person easy as look at them. "I should have been looking where I was going."

"That's okay, child." The old woman's face lightened somewhat, the hint of a smile curling the edges of her mouth. "I'm sure you will not do it again."

Taylor nodded in agreement and backed away, giving Annie a wide berth as she stepped around her, then hurried away, pleased to put some distance between them. She knew witches weren't real. Annie Doucet was just a lonely old woman who lived in a shack. The stories were nothing more than childish nonsense. But even so, she was relieved when she saw Jake's car turn onto Main Street.

When she looked back the sidewalk was empty. The old woman had vanished, as if the whole thing were nothing more than her own imagination. She shuddered and waited for Jake to arrive, a sudden chill running through her despite the warm sunshine.

Chapter 8

JAKE BARLOW STEERED the old Cadillac onto Main Street and came to a stop at the only traffic light in town. He gripped the steering wheel, eager to reach Cassidy's Diner and pick Taylor up. She was seventeen, a year younger than him, and had a body to die for. He drummed his fingers on the dash, willing the light to turn green.

In the back, hidden under a blanket, was a bottle of wine he'd liberated from the refrigerator at home, and a bag of Doritos he'd purchased at the gas station on the way into town. The wine was a cheap Chardonnay with a twist top. He'd panicked for a second after smuggling the booze into the car that he would need a corkscrew and breathed a sigh of relief when he saw the metal cap. He should have known his mother would not buy wine with an actual cork. It surprised him that she even had a bottle of the stuff. Usually box wine was good enough. Hopefully she would not notice it missing, but even if she did, she would probably just assume it hadn't survived one of her all-night binge sessions, which seemed to happen more and more often these days.

Still, it was good luck that he came across it chilling in the fridge. He could not wait to see Taylor's face when she saw it.

Plus, it should loosen her up a bit. Get her nice and relaxed. He grinned, anticipating what might happen when they got up to Sullivan's Pond.

A horn blared behind him. He jumped and glanced up. The light was green. The horn blared again, longer this time.

"Alright. Keep your shirt on." Jake eased the car forward. It backfired and belched a puff of black smoke. He could only imagine what the jackass behind him was thinking now, with the front of his car engulfed in Jake's fumes. He hoped the guy had his window open. It would serve him right for being so impatient.

He cruised down the street, his heart skipping a beat when he saw Taylor waiting at the curb. She was wearing a white cotton blouse and short shorts. The bottoms of the pockets poked out from beneath the denim, the pale fabric contrasting with the smooth sun kissed skin of her legs. He wondered how far up the tan went.

When he pulled up she jumped into the passenger seat, leaning over and kissing him on the cheek. He felt a growing heat in his groin as her breast brushed his elbow.

"Hey."

"Hi." He hoped she had not noticed his reaction to her kiss. "You look nice."

"Thanks. I brought sandwiches." She held up a brown bag. "I didn't want them, but mom insisted."

"At least we won't get hungry." Food was the last thing on Jake's mind. "Why don't you put them in the back."

She twisted around and dropped the bag on the bench seat. "You brought a blanket. Good."

"I didn't think you'd want to sit on the ground." Jake put the car in gear. "Look under it."

She reached back and lifted the blanket, spying the bottle of wine nestled underneath. Her eyes sparkled. "Where did you get that?"

"I bought it." He lied.

"Yeah, right. You stole it from your mom more like."

"Fine. I found it in the fridge." He glanced toward Taylor, taking in the round beauty of her face and hazel eyes that brimmed with excitement. "I thought it would be romantic."

"You're so sweet." She leaned in and gave him another peck on the cheek.

"I know."

"So what are we waiting for? Let's go."

"Right." He pressed the accelerator and pointed the car toward the swimming hole.

Chapter 9

SHERIFF JOHN DECKER drove along the dirt road toward Floyd Benson's camp, watching the trees zip by on both sides. Half a mile later, he passed a weathered hand painted sign nailed to a rotting wooden pole.

NO TRESPASSING - PRIVATE PROPERTY.

Decker ignored the sign and pushed on, passing a junked out car sitting next to a rotten couch that had found its way into the woods, rusty springs poking through the torn fabric. Then he spotted a second notice.

TRESPASSERS WILL BE SHOT.

It seemed Floyd really hated visitors, and Decker knew why. The last thing the old man would want was people nosing around his business, considering what he did up here. Catching him at it was another thing, though.

He pulled into the clearing and climbed from the cruiser, casting an eye around the space, noting the gin still, a mass of pots and copper tubing, under a battered tarp. Next to it stood a stack of empty jugs. There was also a homemade latrine. Further away, a small cabin sat nestled in among the trees. No doubt this was where Floyd lived when he was cooking up his hooch.

He walked over to the ramshackle structure and pulled the door open. A musty, rotting smell greeted his nose, but not much else. He peered in, waiting for his eyes to adjust to the darkness. Inside he saw a bench, a small table, and a cot against the far wall, covered in stained and torn blankets. A kerosene lamp hung from a nail hammered into a roof beam. On the wall, a faded calendar sported a photo of a topless girl astride a Harley. The wording below announced that it was March 2008. The calendar was years out of date. Aside from that, the cabin was empty.

Returning to the center of the clearing, he did a quick three sixty. The place appeared to be abandoned.

"Hello?" Decker shouted out. "Is there anybody around?"

Only the chirping of the birds and the hum of crickets answered him.

"Floyd?" He called to the empty clearing, straining his ears for a reply. "You up here? If you are you'd better come out."

Nothing.

Wherever Floyd Benson might be, he was not here, that much was clear.

Chapter 10

JAKE STEERED the car off the road onto the narrow dirt track that led to Sullivan's Pond. A mile in, the trail dead-ended in a small parking lot. They would have to hike in from here. He pulled up next to a large oak tree and applied the parking brake.

"Here we are." He reached into the back and retrieved the blanket, potato chips, and wine. The alcohol was warm, but it would still be good. They would have to drink it out of the bottle since he had not dared try to sneak wineglasses out of the house, but it was a minor inconvenience. "Should we take these?" He eyed the bag of sandwiches.

"Nah. Leave them here," Taylor said. "We can come back for them if we get hungry."

"Right." Jake opened the car door and jumped out, relishing the feel of the sun on his face. It felt like a hundred degrees.

"It looks like we're the only ones here." Taylor slammed the passenger door and stretched.

"Good. We'll have the place to ourselves." He watched as she lifted her arms in the air, her blouse riding up past her ribs and revealing the bare, silky skin of her belly. Just a little higher and he would catch a peek of her bra.

"Are you checking me out?" Taylor laughed.

"No."

"It's okay if you are." She walked around the car and took the wine. "I'll carry this."

"I wasn't checking you out." Jake felt his face flush with embarrassment. He hadn't realized he was making it so obvious.

"Don't worry about it. I check you out all the time when you have your shirt off."

"You do?"

"Of course." She took his hand in hers. "Come on. I can't wait to dip my feet in the water." She guided him toward the trail that led up to Sullivan's Pond.

THE SWIMMING HOLE was a circular pool of crystal-clear water nestled in a clearing deep in the woods. Fed by a natural spring deep underground, the water was cool and clear, even on the hottest of days.

Jake threw the blanket on the ground and opened it up, making sure there were no pinecones underneath.

Taylor twisted the top off the wine and took a swig, then handed it to him. He gulped some back, trying his best not to cough as it went down.

"So what now?" He gave the wine back to her.

"Well I don't know about you, but I'm going to make myself comfortable." She reached up and undid the top button of her blouse. She moved on to the next, then the next, until the garment fell open. Underneath she wore a pink Bikini top that she'd changed into before he'd picked her up. She slid the blouse from her shoulders and dropped it on the blanket.

"Wow." Jake knew he should look away, but he couldn't. He let his eyes roam from her belly up to the bikini top. "When did you get that?" Last year she had worn a one piece when they came up to the swimming hole, but that was with a group of friends. This time he had her all to himself.

"I bought it at Walmart last week." She sat down on the blanket and motioned for him to do the same. "What do you think?"

He flopped down beside her. "I like it."

"You do?"

"Yes." He looked into her eyes.

"Good. I got it just for you."

"I don't know what to say." His eyes wandered back to her chest.

"Take your tee-shirt off." Taylor took another swig of the wine, gulping it down.

"Why?"

"I want to see what you look like."

"You've seen it before." They had been coming to Sullivan's Pond since they were kids, so it wasn't like he'd never taken his shirt off in front of her.

"Not recently."

"Well, alright." He peeled off his tee, feeling a little self-conscious.

"See, that wasn't so bad."

"I suppose not." Jake took the wine. It was a third empty already. He should have stolen two bottles.

"Come here." Taylor plucked the bottle from his hand and set it aside. She leaned in, her arms snaking around his neck, and pulled him close.

Her lips brushed his in a lingering kiss.

He shivered, a delicious tingle coursing through him.

She kissed him again, harder this time, her lips pressing against his with an urgency that surprised him. When the kiss finally ended she jumped to her feet.

"Let's go swimming."

"Now?" Jake didn't want to go swimming. He wanted to kiss her again.

"Come on. It'll be fun." Taylor kicked off her shoes and unbuttoned her shorts, slipping them down to reveal bikini bottoms. She stepped out of the shorts, pushing them aside. "Still want to stay here?"

"Yes." Jake could not tear his eyes from her slim, tanned body.

"Your loss." Taylor padded to the water. She dipped a foot in. "Yow. It's cold."

"So come back over here." Jake wished she would sit down again. He wanted to keep kissing her.

"I want to swim."

"That water's going to be colder when you get in."

"Only one way to find out." Taylor took a deep breath and stepped from the bank, wading in to the cool, still water. She gasped as the water reached her waist.

"See, I told you," Jake said.

"It's fine. Come on in." Taylor put on her best come hither face. "Please?"

"I can't. I forgot my trunks." They were halfway there by the time he realized he'd forgotten his swimming trunks. He was so engrossed in sneaking the wine out to the car he'd neglected to pick them up on the way out.

"So what?"

"I have nothing to wear."

"Then don't wear anything." Taylor grinned.

"No way. I'm not skinny dipping."

"Aw, come on."

"Nope. Not going to happen."

"I'll go first." Taylor reached around and pulled at the straps of her bikini top, releasing the knot. She held one arm over her chest and pulled the top loose with the other, then threw it back to the shore. "There."

Jake's eyes flew wide. "Wow."

"So, what are you waiting for?"

Jake stared at her for a moment, then his hands fell to his waist. He pulled at the button of his jeans and shook himself out of them, feeling self-conscious standing there in nothing but his undies. He was about to strip those off too, when he paused. A thought had occurred to him. "If I'm going to skinny dip, you have to do the same."

"I am, idiot." Taylor kept her arm over her breasts. "You have my bikini right there."

"I only have the top." His heart was beating a mile a minute.

"No way." She shook her head. "I'm not taking my bottoms off."

"Oh, I see, it's one rule for me, and another for you. You haven't even taken your arm away from your boobs."

"I'm not taking my bottoms off."

"Suit yourself." Jake sat back down on the blanket.

"Fine," Taylor said. "Will this make you happy?" She dropped her arms to her sides, a warm blush spreading across her face.

"It's a start." Jake hopped to his feet, his eyes never straying from Taylor. "I still think you should go the whole hog." He was pushing it, he knew.

"Come on in and maybe I'll let you take them off."

"For real?" He could hardly believe his ears. This was just too good.

"I said it, didn't I?"

That was all it took. Jake reached down and hooked a finger into his briefs, yanked them down.

"Oh, my." Taylor exclaimed; a grin plastered on her face.

Jake knew where she was looking. "Come on. Quit it."

"Well, are you getting in or what?"

Jake didn't need asking twice. He ran to the pond and waded in, gasping when the frigid water hit his skin.

"See, it's not too bad," Taylor said. Her eyes flashed with mischief. "Isn't this better than standing around on the bank?"

"I guess." He ignored his chattering teeth. "So how about it?"

"What?" She was so close he could feel her breath on his neck. It gave him Goosebumps.

"The other half. You said I could take them off."

"I did, didn't I?" She met his gaze. "So, what are you waiting for?"

Chapter 11

DECKER PULLED into the parking lot of the Wolf Haven sheriff's Office, easing the cruiser into the reserved space next to the main door, and killed the engine. He leaned over and reached inside the glove compartment, retrieving the claw he'd pried from the bed of Floyd Benson's truck earlier that day.

He inspected it through the clear plastic of the evidence bag. It was three inches long and curved down to a needlelike point. The inner edge, serrated and sharp, reminding him of a steak knife. Decker did not want to meet whatever animal had lost this.

He pulled on the door release and climbed from the cruiser, then headed toward the office.

When he entered the building, Carol Lawson, Wolf Haven's full-time dispatcher, and de facto desk sergeant, looked up with a smile. "Good morning, John."

"Morning, Carol." After a year asking her to refer to him as Sheriff Decker, at least in the office, he'd given up. It was always going to be John. "Any other calls?"

"Nope. Just the truck."

"Good." He skirted the front counter and made a beeline

for the coffeemaker, throwing the evidence bag on his desk as he went.

"Coffee's fresh not twenty minutes ago. Figured you'd want some caffeine when you came in given how I ruined your morning cup of joe earlier," She said, referencing her call that sent him up to Floyd's abandoned pickup.

"You're an angel." He picked up a coffee cup, inspected the inside to make sure it was clean, and filled it with the dark aromatic liquid.

"What's that?" Carol was eying the evidence bag.

"Don't know. A claw I found stuck in the back of old man Benson's truck."

"Well, that's weird." Carol scooted her chair across the office and picked the bag up.

"You ever see anything like that before?" Decker sat on the edge of his desk.

"Never." She peered at the claw. "Damn thing gives me the creeps. Did you find Floyd?"

"Nope. Not a hair. Found a bunch of his moonshine all over the road, though."

"That should save a few people from going blind."

"No doubt." Decker took a sip of coffee. "You couldn't pay me to drink that stuff. I found his distilling equipment up in the woods. Can you believe he's using an old car radiator as a condenser? Damn fool will end up giving someone lead poisoning. Chad's impounding the thing right now."

"So what about this?" Carol was eying the claw again. "You think it has anything to do with his disappearance?"

"Maybe, maybe not. For all we know Floyd got on the wrong side of another moonshine outfit and they decided to put him out of business."

"That still doesn't explain where he is."

"No, it doesn't." Decker admitted. "He could have gotten scared and hightailed it into the woods, tried to walk back to his camp and gotten lost."

"Or maybe whatever lost this claw got to him." Carol picked the evidence bag up and made a slashing motion. "Do you think he came across a bear?"

"Maybe, although bears are pretty rare in these parts. I can't remember the last time I saw one. If he did, then why would he get out of his truck and confront it in the middle of the night?"

"Maybe he'd been sampling a little too much of his own hooch."

"Maybe." Decker didn't believe Floyd would go head to head with a three hundred pound animal on its own turf, even if he were drunk as a skunk. "If this is a bear, more likely it came across the abandoned truck while foraging for food and decided to check it out."

"So what are you going to do with it?"

"Beats me. I'm not even sure it has anything to do with whatever happened up on Route 16, assuming anything at all happened, and this isn't just a case of Floyd going bat shit crazy on his own whisky." He put the coffee mug to his lips and took a gulp. "If nothing else, it will make a great conversation point at the next town meeting."

Chapter 12

JAKE BARLOW STOOD FACING Taylor Cassidy in the cool waters of the swimming hole. He could hardly believe it. She was actually going to let him go through with it.

"If you don't hurry up, I might change my mind," Taylor said.

The words shook Jake from his stupor. He pushed his hands beneath the water, feeling around until he found her hips. Her skin felt smooth.

He located the strings that held the bikini on, and pulled at the knots, his hands trembling as the flimsy garment came undone. When he lifted his hands from the water, he was holding the prize.

He grinned and threw it toward the water's edge. It missed the bank and landed in the water with a faint plop.

"Good going, genius." Taylor scolded him, although from the tone of her words, she didn't sound too mad. "You'd better get that before it sinks. I don't want to have to ride back to town bare ass."

"You wouldn't be bare ass. You have your shorts." Jake replied. He put his arms around her waist and pulled her toward him, his hands snaking lower down her back. Her breasts brushed against his chest.

"Hey, you're supposed to be rescuing my bikini." She pushed at him playfully.

"In a minute." Jake protested. If the bikini sank, he'd fish it out later. There were better things to do. He leaned in and kissed her.

"That's nice." Taylor mumbled. She ran her hands down his back, and across his bare rump, where they lingered. "I still want my bikini though."

"Come on. Seriously?"

"Yes, seriously," she said, pushing him backward toward the shore. "Go get that bikini."

"Alright, I'm going." Jake splashed toward the bank. "You're a tease."

"Am not."

"Are too."

He reached for the floating garment, plucked it from the water, and tossed it onto dry land. "Happy now?"

"Yep." Taylor ran her hands through her hair. "Grab the wine while you're there."

"What?" All Jake wanted was to do was get back to Taylor. "I'll have to get out of the water."

"So what?"

"You just want to see my naked butt."

"Maybe I do," Taylor agreed. "But I also want the wine."

"Fine." Jake stepped out of the water. He shivered. The water was chilly when he'd gotten in, but now it felt warmer than the air. Worse, he really needed to pee.

"Hurry." Taylor waded closer to the shore, the water lapping just above her hips.

"I need to take a leak." He headed toward the woods. "I'll be back in a second."

"Don't be long." Taylor watched him disappear between the pine trees.

The sudden silence was eerie. She hugged her chest and waited for him to return.

A minute passed, then two.

How long could it possibly take him to relieve himself? She moved toward the bank and scanned the tree line, but there was no sign of him.

"Are you done yet?" She called out, but there was no reply. "Jake?"

She waited another minute, and still he had not returned. A stab of fear gripped her. What if he'd fallen and hurt himself, or a snake had bitten him? She knew that there were poisonous snakes crawling around out here. Spiders, too. Or maybe he'd just wandered further into the woods so she wouldn't see him peeing. He was probably on his way back already, and she would look mighty silly panicking over nothing.

"Jake. Are you alright?" She listened for a reply. None came.

That left only one option. She paddled to the water's edge and stepped out, wishing that Jake would reappear so she didn't have to search for him. She was about to scoop up her bikini and put it on when a voice drifted from the woods.

"Help me."

"Jake?" Taylor's heart skipped a beat.

"Oh God. Help me."

Taylor ran to the edge of the forest. She paused, hesitant to step into the underbrush. "Where are you?"

"Over here. Please, hurry."

"Where?" She could not locate which direction the voice was coming from. It sounded like he was to her right, but now she wasn't sure.

He didn't respond.

"Jake. What's wrong?" She pushed through a gap in the undergrowth and looked around. But there were so many trees, so much scrub, that she could walk right past him if he was two feet away. "I can't see you. Where are you?"

A flock of birds took to the air, the sudden flap of their wings making her jump.

"Jake. Tell me where you are."

"I'm right here." Jake lunged out from behind a fat pine tree.

She screamed and stumbled backwards.

Jake collapsed, laughing. "That was awesome. You should have seen your face."

"Not funny." Taylor's heart was beating out of her chest. "You scared me."

"Come on. It was hilarious."

"No, it wasn't." She punched him, the blow landing on his shoulder. "What were you thinking?"

"It was a joke."

"Well, it was stupid."

"Sorry." He looked her up and down, his eyes lingering on her breasts before they fell lower. He grinned. "It was worth it though."

She remembered her state of undress. A flush of embarrassment washed over her. "Hey, stop that." She covered herself with her arms.

"I was just fooling around. I didn't mean anything by it. I just wanted to get a good look at you," Jake said. "Why don't we get back into the water?"

"I don't want to." Taylor turned toward the clearing, her cheeks burning. He had to ruin everything. "I'm going to get dressed and then you can take me home."

"Really?" Jake sounded disappointed. "Is it because I was checking you out?"

She stomped off, ignoring him.

"I'm naked too. Look, you can check me out."

She glared at him, then turned and walked back to the blanket. She picked through her clothes. The bikini bottoms were too wet to wear, but the shorts and blouse were fine. She dressed and glanced back toward the woods. There was no sign of her boyfriend.

"Jake, come on, quit fooling around. This isn't funny anymore. I want to go home."

"Oh God, oh Jesus. No." The scream came from beyond the trees.

"Really?" Taylor shook her head in disbelief. "This again? Come out here and take me home." She reached down and searched his pants, pulling the car keys from his pocket. "If you don't come out, I'm going to leave you here and you can walk back to town." She jangled the keys in the air.

"Help me." The cry was desperate.

"Alright, that's enough." She marched toward the woods. "You just don't know when to give up, do you?" Any hope he had of ever getting her naked again was diminishing fast. She wasn't even sure she wanted to keep dating him at that moment.

She pushed the brush aside, cursing as a thorn snagged her arm, and entered the forest once more.

It was dark under the canopy. It took a moment for her eyes to adjust to the gloom. When they did, she saw why Jake hadn't followed her back to the swimming hole, and screamed.

Chapter 13

CHAD HARDWICK PULLED a handkerchief from his pocket and wiped away the beads of sweat that were accumulating on his forehead. He wished, not for the first time, that the sheriff would hire another deputy so he didn't have to do all the grunt work himself.

He hefted a large metal boiling pot into the back of the cruiser and slammed the door. It was going to take several trips to disassemble the entire still at this rate. He wondered if he could requisition a truck for the job. It would sure cut down on time. Maybe the sheriff would even let him use Floyd's old beater to haul the junk out of the moonshiner's camp. It wasn't like it was being used for anything else, sitting down at the impound lot like it was. He'd have to get it running first.

He leaned against the car, took a swig of bottled water, and surveyed the clearing.

The place was a dump. The cabin near the trees looked like it might collapse at any moment. The roofline sagged in the middle. The window was an empty frame, the glass long since smashed. A board covered the hole from the inside. Had Floyd built it? He didn't think so. It looked like an old hunting shack. Opposite the cabin a stack of bald tires tilted precariously like some redneck Tower of Babel. Why did people like Floyd feel the need to keep such things? Was he hoping the treads would miraculously come back and render them useful again, or were the number of tires on your property a sign of status? Chad shook his head, baffled, and turned his attention to the only other structure, a latrine made from rotten tarpaulins. A foul smell emanated from the makeshift toilet, carried in his direction by the breeze.

He finished the bottle of water and dropped it back into the car. No point littering. Not that one bottle would make a difference, given the piles of trash lying around. Floyd wasn't paying his maid enough. He chuckled at this and turned back toward the still. There was space enough on the back seat for at least four of the empty alcohol jugs. Then he could head back to town and get lunch. Nancy Cassidy was sure to have a fresh pot of gumbo cooking, full of sausage and shrimp.

As if agreeing with this plan, his stomach growled.

But first, there was work to do.

Chapter 14

TAYLOR SCREAMED.

Jake sat with his back against a tree, chest ripped open. Dead eyes stared back at her. Straddling him, looming over his sprawled body, stood what she first thought was a huge black bear. It wasn't until the beast turned and fixed her with yellow eyes that shone with unnatural fire, that she realized her mistake.

The scream died in her throat.

The creature was no bear. Heavy jaws brimmed with teeth. A hunched back rippled with powerful muscles under leathery dark skin. It looked more like... Taylor could barely comprehend it. A wolf standing erect on thick hind legs.

The beast took a step toward her.

Taylor froze momentarily, her mind processing the impossible scene. Then she was running, crashing through the woods without a thought for the branches that tore at her skin and drew blood from her bare legs.

She fled headlong toward the swimming hole, and then sprinted in the trail's direction, Jake's keys clutched so tight in her hand that her knuckles turned white. For a moment she thought the creature wasn't following, had turned its attention back to Jake, but then she heard the telltale sound of branches breaking. The thud of heavy footfalls. The car was a short distance away, at the other end of the trail. If only she could reach it.

And then her foot snagged a protruding root. If she fell, it would be over. She stumbled, reaching out to steady herself against a tree. Her hand slipped on the smooth bark. She pitched forward. But by some miracle she stayed on her feet.

Behind her, the beast drew closer. She could hear its labored breath as it narrowed the distance between them. She let out a whimper and ran on, regardless. The end of the trail, and the parking lot, came into view. She burst from the path and made a sprint for the car, pushing forward, expecting the beast to catch her at any moment. Lift her from the ground, close those powerful, impossible jaws around her, and bite down. She was almost at the parking area now. The car would be there. Jake's car.

She put on an extra burst of speed, spurred on by the thought of reaching safety. If she could just keep up this pace, she might make it, but Jake's killer was right behind her. There wasn't much time.

She broke through the trees into the parking lot. Jake's car was only a few feet away.

She fumbled with the keys, looking for the correct one, and raced around to the driver's side, pushing the key into the lock. It turned easily, and the door opened with a gratifying thunk. She climbed in and slammed the door just as the beast reached her. It barreled into the car with a thud, rocking the vehicle.

Taylor screamed, shrinking back.

The beast paused, hot breath fogging the window glass. It fixed her with a glowering stare, and in that look, just for a moment, Taylor thought she saw a spark of something. Not humanity, but something else. A flash of intelligence, gone almost as quickly as it had come. She met the creature's gaze, hypnotized by its yellow eyes, until the beast turned away, backing up to take a second shot at the car.

Reality broke through her stupor. She pushed the key into the ignition and turned it.

The car coughed and sputtered.

"Start, you piece of shit." She slammed her fists into the steering wheel.

The beast pounded on the driver's door a second time. The window shattered into a thousand fragments. She shrank back, lifting her hands against the shower of glass.

The creature staggered away, then turned and charged the car again with a high-pitched shriek.

"Come on, please." She begged, turning the key again. If it didn't start this time, she would be dead.

The engine roared to life as the beast hit the car a third time, a wicked, clawed paw reaching through the broken window to drag her out.

She pushed her foot down on the accelerator. The car shot forward. She felt claws scrape her neck, and then she was skidding around. She turned the wheel hard, zigzagging out of the parking area, past the furious creature, and onto the dirt track that led away from Sullivan's Pond.

The car sped along, kicking up a trail of dust and bumping over rocks as it went. When she looked in the rearview mirror, there was no sign of the nightmare creature.

She flew down the narrow track, her wheels crunching dirt and gravel as she went. She glanced nervously toward the trees on each side of the car, expecting the beast to come crashing from the undergrowth at any moment, but it didn't, and for that, she was grateful.

But it changed nothing. Jake was dead. She could hardly believe it, yet she knew it was true. A sob wracked her body. She fought the urge to vomit. But she didn't have time for that. Besides, there was no way she was stopping the car until she reached town. With tears streaming down her face and a tight lump in her throat, she drove on, putting as much distance as she could between herself and the murderous creature that had torn her boyfriend apart.

Chapter 15

CHAD PARKED up and climbed from the cruiser. He was about to walk toward the Sheriff's Office when a beaten up old Cadillac almost ran him over. He barely saw the car in time to jump out of its path.

The car screeched to a halt.

He swore. Whoever was behind the wheel just earned themselves a reckless driving citation. He rounded the car, pulling his sunglasses from his pocket as he went, and putting them on. The Ray-Bans made him look mean. Authoritative. Plus, people couldn't see his eyes, so he could check out their stuff without giving himself away.

He was about to tap on the window when he realized there was no window, just a space where it should have been. A heavy dent had crushed the driver's side door. The car looked like a bulldozer had gone to work on it.

Taylor Cassidy was behind the wheel, her eyes red and puffy. There was a bloody scratch on the side of her neck. Tears streamed down her face. She was shaking.

"Miss Cassidy?" Chad approached the car, no longer concerned with traffic tickets. "Were you in an accident?"

She looked up at him as if she barely recognized him.

"Do you need help?" Chad said, realizing how stupid the question was even as he uttered the words.

He reached out and pulled on the car door. It wouldn't open. He pulled again, this time putting his foot on the body of the car to provide leverage. The door gave way with a metallic groan, swinging open and almost sending him tumbling to the ground. He regained his balance. "Are you hurt?"

"No." She shook her head. "It's Jake."

"What about Jake?" He reached down and took her arm, helping her out. "Is he okay?"

"No." She collapsed into his arms, head on his chest. Tears flowed down her face. She sounded terrified. She pulled her head from his chest, looked up at him with wide, frantic eyes. "He's dead. A monster killed him."

Chapter 16

DECKER HAD BARELY FINISHED WRITING up his report on Floyd's abandoned truck when the front door burst open, banging back against the wall with a thud that rattled the front window.

"What in god's name." He turned from the computer to see Chad bearing down on him with Taylor Cassidy supported in his arms.

"We've got a problem, boss." Chad said. "I found Miss Cassidy out front in Jake Townsend's Cadillac. Damn thing looks like it got in an argument with an eighteen-wheeler."

Decker jumped to his feet. Carol hopped off her chair. They reached Chad and the hysterical teenager at the same time.

"Bring her through." Decker slipped an arm under Taylor's and together he and Chad maneuvered her toward a chair. "Sit her down here."

As soon as she was in the chair Decker kneeled down. "Taylor honey. Tell me what's going on."

"It's Jake." Taylor's voice quivered when she spoke. Her face was white, and she was shaking like a leaf.

Decker looked up at Chad and Carol, then back to Taylor. "Tell me what happened, Taylor. Can you do that?"

For a moment she appeared to be looking through him as if she had not heard him. Then she took a shaky breath and spoke.

"Jake. Something attacked him. A monster." She broke down, tears streaming down her face. She spoke again, the hysteria in her voice growing. "You have to do something. I'm so scared."

Decker placed his hand on Taylor's arm. "You need to calm down." He stroked strands of hair from her face. "Where is he, Taylor? Where's Jake?"

"Don't let it get me. Oh god, please don't let it get to me." Her eyes were wild. She tried to stand up, but Decker put a hand on her shoulder and guided her back down to the seat.

"Taylor, I need you to take a deep breath. Where is Jake?"

"Sullivan's Pond. We were swimming. He was fooling around, and then it attacked him. It killed him." Tears streamed down her face.

Decker exchanged a glance with Chad and then turned back to Taylor. "What did, Taylor?"

"I don't know. It looked kind of like a wolf, but it wasn't. It was so much bigger. You need to go up there before it escapes. You need to shoot it. Oh Jesus, the things it was doing to him." She sobbed. "You need to kill it."

"We will, Taylor." Decker motioned Chad to get the guns. "Now you stay here with Carol and she will look after you."

Chad sprinted toward the firearms locker. He took out a key and unlocked it. Carol was already on the radio dispatching paramedics to Sullivan's Pond.

Taylor spoke again. "It chased me, it tried to kill me too. If I didn't have Jake's car keys it would have gotten me."

"Can you describe what you saw?"

"I don't know." She sobbed. "It was big, and it walked on

two legs. It had these awful yellow eyes, when it looked at me I knew it wanted to kill me," she howled.

"Alright, Taylor. Carol is going to call your mother and have her come over here and pick you up." He stood up. "We're going to go up to Sullivan's Pond and look around. Where did this happen, Taylor? Was it by the water?"

"No, in the woods. He went to the bathroom. Please tell me you're going to kill it?" She pleaded. "I'm so scared."

"You're safe now." Decker turned to Carol. "Keep an eye on her, will you?"

"Sure thing." Carol kneeled down next to Taylor and stroked her face, clearing the hair from her eyes.

Chad came up behind Decker and handed him a shotgun. "Been a long time since we've needed these."

"Tell me about it." Decker took the weapon. "You good to go?"

"Just say the word." Chad stuffed several extra rounds into his shirt pocket and offered a handful to Decker.

"Then let's go see what we're dealing with." Decker walked toward the door, then turned back to Carol. "Can you tell those paramedics to hold back? Make sure they don't go up to the swimming hole until we get there. Just to be safe." With that, he pulled the door open and stepped out into the bright sunshine of what should have been a perfect summer day.

Chapter 17

THE AMBULANCE WAS WAITING when Decker and Chad arrived at the parking area below Sullivan's Pond. The sheriff pulled up next to the idling vehicle and killed the engine. The two cops climbed from the car and retrieved their hats from the back seat. Chad took the Ray Bans from his pocket and put them on.

Decker rounded the back of the vehicle, opened the trunk of the cruiser and pulled out the shotguns. He kept one for himself and handed the other gun to the deputy.

Next he turned to the paramedics, giving them instructions. "Stay here until we need you." There was no way he was going to let unarmed civilians wander around up at the swimming hole until he knew what they were dealing with.

His mind flashed back to the claw he had pulled from the bed of Floyd's truck. Were the two incidents connected? He hoped not, but Decker didn't believe in coincidence.

"Ready?" he asked Chad, a grim look on his face.

"Sure thing." Chad raised his shotgun and checked that the safety was off. "Whenever you are."

"Keep your eyes peeled. We don't know what we're going

to find up there." Decker moved off in the direction of the trail with Chad following close behind.

Before long the trees closed in around them, blocking out the sun. They moved with caution, ready for whatever might wait in the woods. The path was narrow, with tall pines and dense undergrowth on both sides. It was perfect cover for an animal, even a large one, to hide out. Above them, in the thick canopy, birds twittered, calling back and forth among themselves, and crickets chirped happily in the brush. Insects buzzed around the officers as they pushed forward. Everything was normal. Tranquil. Except for the terrified kid back at the sheriff's station.

Decker scanned the terrain ahead, looking for any sign of whatever put the fear of god into Taylor Cassidy, but saw nothing out of the ordinary.

When they reached the swimming hole, it didn't take long to find evidence of the teenager's activities.

"Looks like they were having quite the party." Decker picked up the half empty bottle of wine.

"You're telling me." Chad was eyeing the pile of clothes. "Guess they fancied a little skinny dipping."

"Teenagers." Decker muttered. "This is why I don't have kids."

"Right. You never fooled around when you were young?"

"That was different."

"Sure it was." Chad grinned.

Decker shot the deputy a look. "Let's keep focused on the job at hand, shall we?" His thoughts turned to Taylor. By now Carol had surely called Nancy. She'd gone through so much already, what with her husband skipping out on them and leaving her to run the diner all by herself, and then Taylor's troubles at school. Not that the girl was a bad kid, just acting out. It had been a tough few years, and now, just when things seemed to improve, this happened. He would drop by and check on them later. But right now there was a missing kid to find.

"Taylor said Jake went off to pee," Chad said, looking around. "We should probably search the woods. There's no sign of him down here."

"Good idea." Decker examined the area, his eyes roaming the tree line. Everything looked normal, nothing out of place. He put the bottle back down on the ground and started toward the trees, walking along the edge of the woods until he saw a path through the tangle of undergrowth that pushed out from between the pines.

He stepped into the pinewoods, following the trail as it meandered between the trees. He wondered how many kids had come up here to make out over the years. The swimming hole had been a popular spot to bring a girl since he'd been a teen. It was where he'd taken Nancy the night of the senior prom. They'd snuck up the dark trail to the water and made a campfire out of twigs and branches he collected. He'd lost his virginity that night in almost the same spot that Taylor and Jake had laid their blanket out. Judging by the copious amount of trash that littered the ground, he had to assume the popularity of the spot had not waned.

He spotted a crushed beer can; the printing faded and unreadable, and then another. A few feet further, a candy bar wrapper half covered by dirt.

It was what he saw next that made him stop in his tracks.

Chad came up behind him, a look of horror on his face.

Jake lay across the path, his body twisted at an impossible angle, his glazed eyes staring past the trees toward the sky. He was naked, his pale skin mired in dried blood. A gaping hole marked where the boy's stomach should have been. A mess of guts spilled out onto the ground, attracting a swarm of blowflies that buzzed in haphazard circles. His mouth was open in a frozen death scream.

Decker took a deep breath, fighting the urge to turn and

run. He lifted the shotgun, aware that whatever had eviscerated Jake could still lurk unseen within the trees.

He turned to Chad. "Better get the crime scene tape from the car, and notify the M.E., tell them to get up here." He kneeled and examined the wounds, ignoring the pungent odor that assaulted his nostrils. "And tell the paramedics to stand down. Doesn't look like we'll be needing their services today."

Chapter 18

JEREMIAH BOUDREAUX PACED BACK and forth inside his trailer on Black Bayou Road, a few miles north of Wolf Haven. He was not a happy man. He still hadn't found his son Terry, and he needed someone to drive a load of scrap out to the junkyard in Bogalusa. He would have made the trip himself, but he had already spent the entire morning over at the landfill hauling whatever metal he could find into the back of his pickup.

It was illegal to scavenge the mounds of trash. There were signs at intervals warning folk that removing items from the landfill was an offense punishable by a fine of up to $500 or three days in jail, but that was just stupid. Why leave valuable stuff to rot, when he could sell it for cold hard cash.

He'd bribed the guard at the gate, of course, just like he did every Saturday morning. Slipped him a ten. After that he was free to wander among the piles of waste, looking for rusty gold. Today he'd found two old washing machines, an iron grate, and some industrial shelf units with buckled legs. It was a good haul, but now his back ached. Washing machines were heavy, and since Terry had not come home last night Jeremiah had to lift them into the truck all by himself.

Now the last thing he wanted was to spend a couple more hours driving everything over to the junkyard, but he needed the cash, not to mention the fact that if he didn't get it unloaded, there would be no room in the back for the consignment of gently used tires he was picking up first thing Monday morning.

"Shit." He shouted the word for no other reason than to make himself feel better. It was all Floyd's fault. If the old man had not offered Terry work running illegal booze half way around the state, then he wouldn't need to do all this stuff by himself. Hell, it wasn't like Floyd was even family, at least not to him. A brother-in-law was not blood. Not that he even held that title anymore. Jeremiah had divorced Pamela, Floyd's sister, five years ago, and yet the man still hung around like a bad smell.

He picked up a bottle and downed a mouthful of the clear liquid inside. It burned as it made its way to his stomach. At least there was one benefit to Terry working for Floyd. Jeremiah got all the free hooch he wanted, and he had to admit, for all his flaws, the old man knew how to make liquor.

That didn't do Jeremiah an ounce of good when there was a load to deliver.

There was nothing for it. He would have to go up to Floyd's camp and find his son, who was probably sleeping off yet another drinking session with Floyd after their midnight run. Quality control. That's what the pair of them jokingly called it. It was laughable. It was also a regular occurrence these days and a turn up that Jeremiah found mildly distasteful, not because he disapproved of such things, but more because he wasn't a part of them.

He found the keys to the truck, grabbed the bottle of moonshine and stomped outside, the bright daylight hurting his eyes and causing him to squint until he adjusted to it.

He climbed behind the wheel, gunned the engine, and set off toward Floyd's land.

It only took Jeremiah a few minutes to drive the three miles to the moonshiner's camp. Along the way he swigged the alcohol and then pushed the bottle down between the seats as his destination came into view.

He pulled up next to the cabin and climbed from the truck.

There was no one in sight.

"Terry?" He called out. When he didn't receive an answer, he poked his head inside the cabin, but it was empty.

"Terry. You up here?" He wandered toward the still. "Floyd?"

It was not like the old moonshiner to leave his equipment in full view. He hadn't even pulled the tarps down over it, the fool.

He reached the still and looked around. He had been hoping there might be some more booze up here, maybe a couple of jugs lying around for the taking, but he saw only empties. That wasn't the only thing he saw. The alcohol still was half pulled apart, tubes dangling where the main pot should have been. There was a sheet of paper stuck to the ruined apparatus.

Jeremiah leaned close and read it, the header in large bold type telling him all he needed to know.

WOLF HAVEN SHERIFF'S OFFICE
NOTICE OF IMPOUNDMENT

He read the rest of the notice and sighed. No wonder Terry hadn't come home last night. The damn fool had gone and gotten himself arrested for running Floyd's illegal liquor.

There was no point in hanging around. He would go down to the sheriff's office and bail the stupid kid out the first chance he got. In the meantime, he needed to pee.

Jeremiah ambled over to the latrine, taking a deep breath to avoid breathing in the fumes given off by the nasty combination of rotting shit and piss for as long as he could. Despite this, the acrid smell still worked its way up his nose.

He unzipped his pants and peed, watching the arc of yellow liquid splash down into the hole. Then he zipped himself up again, thankful to escape the nasty tent.

He was about to pull the flap back and head toward his truck, when he realized he was no longer alone. Someone was walking around the camp, and they weren't being quiet about it either.

Jeremiah froze, unsure what to do.

Maybe Floyd and Terry hadn't gotten hauled off to jail. If they noticed the cops coming up the dirt road, they might have ducked into the woods and waited until the coast was clear before coming out.

Or it could be the sheriff and his half-baked deputy coming back to clean out the rest of the equipment. The last thing Jeremiah wanted to do was end up sharing a cell with Floyd and Terry. Then who would bail them out? Not Pamela, that was for sure. She was still holding a grudge after catching him in the back of his truck with Ruby Wells from the discount grocery store in Hodgenville, two towns over. Five years and she still couldn't forgive him. It wasn't like she was pure as driven snow either. He'd known all about her brief liaisons with Matt Barker up at Hardee's Gas on Route 4. That man sure filled her up in more ways than one. Jeremiah would have chuckled at that under normal circumstances, but since he was holed up in a stinking latrine hiding from Sheriff Decker, he didn't.

Instead, he stood not daring to move, doing his best not to breathe, partly for fear of discovery, and also because he didn't want to breathe in any more of Floyd's shit fumes than necessary.

The footsteps were right outside the tent. He heard a sniff, like a dog checking out a scent, then another. Did the sheriff have a K-9 unit now?

He recoiled, expecting the tarps to part at any second, and the sheriff to haul him off to jail, either for trespassing, or for being one of Floyd's accomplices. That didn't happen though. Instead, the footsteps receded until there was nothing but silence outside the latrine. Whoever was poking around had gone.

Jeremiah lingered, hidden by the tarpaulins, for a few more minutes, until he felt it was safe to move, then he parted the flaps and slipped from the toilet, relieved to be back out in the open air.

The camp was empty.

There was no sign anyone had been there. The partly dismantled distillation apparatus was the same as before, complete with the impound notice. His truck still waited next to the cabin.

It occurred to him that if the cops had been here, then his pickup, sitting out in the open for all to see, would be a dead giveaway. All Sheriff Decker needed to do was call in the plate number and his goose was well and truly cooked.

Whoever he heard walking around, it was obviously not the police.

Regardless, he should probably make himself scarce. He didn't want to push his luck. Decker would return at some point to get the rest of the impounded equipment, and Jeremiah didn't want to be around when he did.

He hurried toward his truck, retrieving his keys from his pocket as he went. He was five feet from the vehicle when he stopped short, his eyes alighting on something strange in the soft dirt. A set of paw prints moving across the camp. Tracks that Jeremiah did not recognize as any animal he was familiar with, which was odd considering how much time he spent out in the woods hunting. He bent to inspect the weird impressions. They looked somewhat like a barefooted human had strolled through the camp, except they were too big, much too big. Worse, he could see holes where claws had penetrated the ground.

He looked around, nervous, but there was no sign of the owner of the footprints. That didn't make Jeremiah feel any better, because he'd noticed something else. The birds no longer sang in the trees. The woods had fallen silent. It was eerie, disturbing. A shiver ran up his spine.

He ran to the pickup and slammed the door. He pushed the key into the ignition and started the engine, pushed the gearstick into first, hoping that whatever was prowling around didn't hear the metallic grind from the worn gearbox. Then he was moving, putting as much distance between himself and the camp as he could.

Chapter 19

DECKER WATCHED the M.E. poke and prod the corpse of Jake Barlow. Not for the first time in the last few hours, he repressed the urge to vomit. In all his years in law enforcement, he had never seen a body quite so torn up and mangled. He wished he were somewhere else, anywhere else. This was not the kind of messed up shit he had signed up for. Fist fights at the County Line Saloon, domestic disputes, and the occasional drunk and disorderly, that was more his speed these days. In the five years since taking the sheriff's job and returning to his hometown, he'd never even pulled his gun. Not once. This was a quiet place, a simple place. That was the way he liked it, and now this.

He watched the forensic photographer, called in from New Orleans, as he darted around, snapping pictures of the ground surrounding the body, the woods, and the trail, anything he could point his lens at. The man had already spent half an hour documenting the pile of clothes and the blanket by the water, and a further forty minutes photographing the body from every conceivable angle, before the M.E. went to work. Decker wondered if they needed so many photographs or if the man was just keeping himself busy to avoid looking at the bloody mess that had been a healthy, horny teenager only a few hours ago.

His mind wandered to another time, many years before, when he was still a kid. The day his mother died. He wondered if his father, himself the sheriff of Wolf Haven, had stood and looked upon a similar scene out in the woods behind their house. What his mother was doing out beyond the tree line, deep in the forest, no one knew, but when they found her there was no mistaking the cause of death. They blamed a wild dog, said she must have crossed paths with it while out walking on a hot summer day. But his father, the first person on the scene, didn't believe that. He spent the next eight years growing more and more obsessed with finding out the truth, or at least the truth as he imagined it to be. He followed leads, most of which went nowhere, spent hours in the pinewoods looking for any sign of the animal that killed his wife, and slowly but surely alienated his son. When Decker was eighteen, he left for college and was happy to be away from the old man. Six months later his father died, swallowing enough pills to strike down a horse.

"Still at it?" Chad's voice brought Decker back to the present. He looked up to see the deputy trudging toward him from the direction of the swimming hole, now strung with yellow crime scene tape all the way from the head of the trail.

"Seems to be." Decker said. He turned away from the body and rubbed his neck, swatting away a mosquito that was trying to score a free lunch. "This has turned into one crappy day."

"Sure has." Chad said. He held up a wallet in a plastic evidence bag. "We have a positive ID on the kid. There was a driver's license in his jeans. It's Jake Barlow alright."

"Figured as much."

"Who's going to tell the parents?"

"I'll swing by on the way back to town, break the news. Damned if I know what to tell them though," Decker said.

"Right." Chad sounded relieved.

"Sheriff Decker?" The M.E. pushed her way through the brush, her eyes cold and haunted despite the forced smile on her lips. She pulled off the blue latex gloves she was wearing as she approached, then proffered her hand to Decker. For a moment he paused, reluctant to shake a hand that had spent the last 60 minutes probing a corpse, but then he took it and shook.

"So, what do we have?" Decker asked.

"Well, what we are looking at is severe trauma. A tremendous amount of damage to the neck, chest. The stomach is flayed open with organs chewed and removed. There are defensive wounds to the arms and legs. Whatever did this inflicted the damage perimortem."

"Huh?" Chad looked confused.

"Perimortem. Right before death," the M.E. explained. "He was still alive, at least to begin with. Poor kid."

"Oh. Right." Chad looked pale.

"Cause of death?" Decker asked.

The M.E. nodded. "Acute blood loss and shock. He wouldn't have lasted long. There were several major arteries torn. But I imagine you're talking about what attacked him rather than what the physical cause of death was, am I right?"

"Right."

"I'd say a large animal. There are bite marks around the neck and chest areas, not to mention deep lacerations to the arms and legs from the animal's claws. I'll give you a more definitive answer when I get the body into the lab and I can compare the marks to known predators. Measure the jaw size and bite radius. Although based on my preliminary findings, I'm stumped about what could have done this."

"Could a bear be responsible?"

"Possible, but unlikely given the scarcity of bears in these parts. And despite what people think, fatal bear attacks are rare, less than three or four a year nationwide. You're more likely to get struck by lightning."

"A wolf then?" Decker asked, remembering Taylor's vague description.

"There are no wolves in Louisiana anymore. They've been officially extinct since the eighties. Now a coyote, that's another matter. They aren't indigenous to the area, but they are around. An invasive species."

"So a coyote could have done this?"

"This amount of damage? It would surprise me."

"And yet here we are." Decker's eyes drifted to the corpse. For a moment it wasn't Jake Barlow lying dead on the ground, but Decker's mother. He looked away again quickly.

"Like I said, I'll have more information after I conduct the autopsy. In the meantime, I would suggest you keep the good folk of Wolf Haven out of the woods. Bear or not, something ripped chunks out of this poor boy."

Chapter 20

CAROL LAWSON RUBBED her temples to ease the headache that refused to go away despite several aspirins. At first, after Decker and Chad rushed up to the swimming hole, she harbored a faint hope that Taylor might be mistaken about Jake - that they might find him alive - but the sheriff put that notion to rest when he radioed to report their gruesome discovery.

She popped yet another aspirin and watched Nancy help Taylor into a waiting car in the parking lot. It had taken two hours to calm the hysterical girl enough for her mother to take her home, and even now Taylor was barely functioning.

Nancy climbed into the car and reversed out from the parking space. Carol closed her eyes, praying the headache would subside. No sooner had she done so than the front door opened. When she opened her eyes she found Jeremiah Boudreaux standing at the counter.

"I've come to get my boy." Jeremiah said.

"I'm sorry?" Carol replied.

"Terry. I'm here to bail him out." Jeremiah glanced around the office. "You have him in your jail?"

"We don't have anyone out back right now." Carol wondered why Jeremiah thought his son was there.

"Well, he ain't been home since last night, so if he ain't here then where the hell is he?"

Carol shook her head. "I really don't know."

"Well, you should. Your impound notices are all over Floyd's still."

"Terry was with Floyd Benson?"

"Sure was," Jeremiah said. "Not doing anything illegal, mind you, just helping the old man move some old tires down to the dump."

Sure he was, thought Carol. So it was Terry who was with Floyd in the truck last night. "We found Floyd's truck abandoned up on Route 16. You wouldn't know anything about that would you?"

"Hell no. What do you mean you found Floyd's truck abandoned?"

"Exactly what I said. It was just sitting there, right in the middle of the road with the keys still in it and hooch bottles smashed all over. I think the sheriff might want to talk to you when he gets back."

"Why?" Jeremiah looked startled. "I haven't done nothing wrong. I don't know nothing about any liquor bottles."

"I'm not saying you've done anything wrong, Mr. Boudreaux, but if Terry was with Floyd, and you haven't seen him since, then we have two people missing."

"Missing? Why would they be missing? More than likely they went off and got roaring drunk out in the woods."

Carol wondered if she should tell Jeremiah about the animal attack, but thought better of it. Given the discovery of the claw in the back of the truck, she had a growing suspicion that whatever had attacked Jake might have been up on Route 16 the previous evening. If that was the case they had a real problem, and maybe two more victims. "Did you want to report Terry missing?"

"Hell no. Stupid kid is probably sleeping off a hangover somewhere," Jeremiah said. "He'll come back when he's good and ready."

"Your call," Carol said. She rubbed her forehead again. Her headache was getting worse.

Chapter 21

BY THE TIME Decker returned to Wolf Haven, the sun was slipping low on the horizon.

After leaving the swimming hole, he drove to the Barlow residence to tell them of their son's death, watching as their faces turned from disbelief to anguish. It was never easy being the bearer of bad news, and it was worse given Jake's age. Afterward, he felt drained and empty. He checked in with Chad, who was still at Sullivan's Pond until the M.E. removed the body, and then drove the short distance back to town.

As soon as he entered the Sheriff's Office he went to his desk drawer and removed the claw found in the bed of Floyd's truck. He turned it over, examining it. When Carol filled him in on her conversation with Jeremiah Boudreaux, his unease grew. Had the moonshiners stumbled across the same animal that attacked Jake Barlow? It would explain the strange claw. It would also mean there were two more victims in the woods. It was too dark to do anything about that right now. It would have to wait until morning.

"What are we going to do?" Carol asked at length.

"Nothing, tonight," Decker replied. He held up the claw.

"Still, I'd love to know what kind of animal we're dealing with."

"I'll put a call in to the university and see if they have anyone that can help us identify it."

"Good idea. We should know more when the autopsy results come back for Jake Barlow. The M.E. said she'd send her report over as soon as she had something. Maybe that will give us some clue what we're dealing with here."

"What about the missing moonshiners?"

"We'll start a search at first light," Decker said. "I hate to say it, but I think I know what we'll find."

"We'll need to let folk know what's going on," Carol said. "We don't want another attack."

"I agree. Not that we can say much. Best guess is a bear. The medical examiner thinks it's unlikely, but we have to say something. Why don't you give Channel 6 a call. Don't give them too many specifics, though. Just say we have a bear on the prowl. People should stay indoors and steer clear of the woods."

"I'll get right on it."

"In the meantime, I'm going to check on Nancy and Taylor." He dropped the claw back in the drawer, picked up his hat, and headed for the door.

"John?" Carol called after him. "Before you go—"

"I know what you're going to say." Decker turned back toward her. "You don't need to."

"This attack, this whole nasty business," Carol said. "I just want to make sure you're coping okay?"

"What happened to my mother has nothing to do with this. That was a long time ago."

"But it must have brought back memories." Carol looked concerned. "You left Wolf Haven because of your mother's death, and what it did to your family."

"I left to go to college."

"We both know that's not true. You couldn't cope with the change in your father. His obsessions."

"And I made my peace. I came back."

"Almost two decades later," Carol said. "I'm worried about you, John. What you went through back then was horrific, and now with Jake being killed like this—"

"I'm handling it just fine." Decker reassured her, pulling the door open. "There's no need to worry." But even as he said the words, he didn't believe them. Memories were stirring, and for the first time in years, he felt the pain of those dark days from so long ago.

Chapter 22

JEREMIAH BOUDREAUX DROVE BACK to his trailer in a black mood. Now and then he pried the bottle of illegal liquor from between the driver and passenger seat and took a long swig. By the time he got home, the bottle was empty.

He stumbled to the trailer and pulled the door open, foraging around until he found a second bottle, unscrewed the top, and went to work on it. There was still no sign of Terry, and he still had a full load of scrap in the bed of his pickup. He would have to make the trip to the junkyard on Monday, which would cost him a bundle since he'd planned on hauling a load of old tires for recycling. Now he would not be able to. It was a good thing Terry had not shown his face. When he did, he would be in for it. Stupid kid.

He slumped down on the old couch that he'd found years before on the side of the road and turned on the TV, flicking through channels until he found a black and white John Wayne movie.

His thoughts turned to Floyd. If that sheriff's dispatcher was right, the old man was missing too. Not surprising, since the cops had impounded his liquor operation. For sure, the moonshiner had holed up in the woods, hiding out to avoid a stint in county jail. He'd probably stay out there a while. If anyone knew the pine forest, it was Floyd. As for his son, Terry would come home when he was good and ready, probably when the booze ran low. And when he did, he'd get a good hiding.

As for Sheriff Decker, there was no way Jeremiah was going to give him any information. Not on your life. Damn cops, always poking their noses in where they didn't belong. Only last year Jeremiah had spent four days in a cell on a drunk and disorderly thanks to Decker. It wasn't the first time either. It was like the sheriff had it in for him. That dispatcher sure seemed jumpy, though, when he'd said Terry hadn't come home. And he had to admit that it was odd, Floyd leaving his truck like that, and breaking all those jugs of liquor. He'd known the old man for years, and in all that time Floyd had never abandoned a load.

He put the bottle to his lips again and gulped back a good amount of alcohol. His eyes felt heavy. A dull warmth closed in around him. Soon he'd forgotten all about Floyd and the abandoned truck.

The bottle fell from his grip and landed on the floor, the clear liquid seeping out onto the carpet as Jeremiah snored.

Chapter 23

SHERIFF DECKER PARKED outside Cassidy's diner, pulling into a space between Taylor's car, which had not moved since that morning, and a blue Toyota that he did not recognize, and climbed from his cruiser. The place was dark, a closed sign hanging in the window. Normally the restaurant would be open for at least another hour, but Nancy had better things to do tonight than feed the town of Wolf Haven.

He skirted the building, walking down the driveway at the side of the diner until he saw the house silhouetted against the pinewoods beyond. The kitchen light was on, but there were no other outward signs anyone was home. He knew Nancy was there, though. Her red SUV was parked near the front steps.

He knocked. A second later there was movement, and a voice drifted from inside.

"Who is it?"

"Sheriff Decker."

The door opened. Nancy stood there dressed in a pair of old jeans and a baggy tee. "John. Come in."

He stepped over the threshold. "How's Taylor?"

"How do you think?" Nancy closed the door. "She was

hysterical when I brought her home. Couldn't stop crying. I found some sleeping pills in the cabinet and gave her a couple. I'm not sure it was the right thing to do, but it worked. She's resting now."

"Good." He followed her into the kitchen. "She's a tough kid, she'll get through it."

"I hope so."

"She will." He reached into his pocket and brought out a cell phone. "I thought she might want this back. We found it up at Sullivan's Pond." He paused, unsure if he should mention what else they found up at the swimming hole, and then decided against it. There was no need to mention the discarded bikini. It was irrelevant now.

"Thanks. I thought you might need it for evidence." Nancy took the phone and placed it down on a side table.

"Unnecessary," Decker said, "Besides, I know where to find it if something comes up."

"Of course." Nancy said, her eyes on Decker.

"She's a lucky girl." He met Nancy's gaze, and for a moment he wondered why he'd ever left town. Why he'd left her.

"She is, I know. Did you find Jake?"

He nodded. "Just like Taylor said. Kid didn't stand a chance. I spoke to the parents this afternoon."

Nancy sighed. "Those poor people."

"It could have been worse. If Taylor hadn't gotten out of there so fast…"

"I don't want to think about that." Nancy shuddered. "Do you know what attacked them?"

"A wild animal of some sort, although I couldn't begin to guess what it is," Decker said. "We'll know more once we get the report back from the M.E. In the meantime, we're telling folk it was a bear."

"A bear?" Nancy shook her head. "That doesn't match what Taylor described at all."

"I know that, but I don't have another suspect."

"What about a wolf?"

"People are more likely to believe a bear than a wolf. Unlikely as either scenario sounds."

"I can't believe this is happening." Nancy looked up at Decker. A tear rolled down her cheek.

"It'll be alright." Decker hesitated a moment, then took her in his arms.

"I'm so pleased you're here." She fell against him and put her head on his shoulder. "It makes me feel safe."

He ran a hand through her thick red hair, noticing for the first time the faint flecks of hazel in her deep blue eyes. "I won't let anything happen to you," he said, holding her close.

"Good." She reached up, sliding her hands around his neck, and then she kissed him, her lips brushing his. He froze for a moment, surprised, and then returned her kiss with fervor. For a moment the years fell away, and he was eighteen again. He pulled her close, determined not to waste this chance the way he had all those years before.

She broke away, a faint smile upon her face. "I've wanted to do that for such a long time."

"Me too." He kissed her again, his lips lingering on hers, wanting the moment to last forever.

For a long while, they held each other in a comforting embrace, Decker stroking her hair, and Nancy holding him tight, feeling safe and comfortable in his arms.

"I don't want to be alone tonight. Stay with me?" Her voice was soft, barely more than a whisper.

Decker looked at her. "I'm not sure I should."

"Why, because you're the sheriff?"

"No, because with everything that's happened, I don't want to take advantage."

"You're not."

"What about Taylor?" Decker asked. The girl had been

through hell, and the last thing he wanted to do was make the situation worse.

"She's resting. I doubt she'll even notice you're here. Besides, I'm sure she'd feel safer knowing you were close by." She took his hand and led him through the house, toward the bedroom, closing the door.

"Nancy, before we go any further, maybe we should talk."

"Not now." Nancy said, her voice low and urgent.

"Last time we were together, things didn't end right. I owe you—"

"I need this, John. I need you, here and now. The past is nothing but memories."

"But—"

"Shut up." She lifted her top up and off and then threw it to one side. She wore nothing underneath.

Decker stepped close, took her in his arms, kissed her again.

Then they were on the bed, bodies joined in a fit of passion. Their lovemaking was fast and heated, a blur of wild need. Afterward, they made love again, and now it was gentle. They rediscovered each other, explored each other in a way they hadn't for years. Afterward, they lay together for the longest time without speaking. Decker held Nancy close, his hand stroking the small of her back. She rested her head on his chest, her auburn hair spilling across him, and fell asleep.

Chapter 24

THERE WAS ONLY one customer left by the time Ed Johnson, owner of The County Line Saloon, announced last call. Benny Townsend, proprietor and sole employee of the Pump and Go gas station on the south side of town, looked up at the TV above the bar, half watching a news story about a local kid killed by a bear in the pinewoods outside of town.

"Nasty business," he said, shaking his head. He offered his beer glass to Ed. "I'll take one for the road."

"Sure." Ed took the glass and refilled it. He glanced toward the TV. "What are the odds?"

"Beats me." Benny pushed four crumpled dollar bills across the bar. "They say a bear did it."

"A bear," Ed scoffed, pushing the refilled glass toward Benny. "In all the years I've lived here, I've never once seen a bear."

"Me either." Benny lifted the glass and downed half the drink in one gulp. "It makes no sense."

"Not a lick." Ed leaned on the bar and watched Benny drain his glass. "One more?"

"Nah." Benny heaved himself to his feet, pulling a stained

jacket from the barstool. "I'm off. Got to be up early tomorrow."

"Right. You take care on the way home." Ed looked past his friend, to the empty bar beyond. It had been a slow night, but he was glad it was over. "Make sure that bear doesn't get you."

"Nothing's gonna get me," Benny chuckled. He turned away and took a stumbling step toward the front door. "I'm too old and too scrawny to be worth the time."

Ed watched him lurch across the barroom and slip out into the night. He went to the sound system and flicked a switch, killing the music. Next he made a quick circuit around the bar, collecting empty glasses and wiping down the tables.

He wrinkled his nose. The place smelled like cigarette smoke despite his no smoking policy. People always snuck one in rather than stand outside in the humid night air. That was fine. He couldn't afford to turn business away, and would not even bother with the non-smoking thing at all except for his asthma, which had gotten worse over the last few years.

He stacked the glasses in the dishwasher, wiped the bar down, and reached up to turn off the TV. On the screen was a picture of a storm churning in the Gulf of Mexico, twin spiral arms spinning around the calm center as it moved toward land.

Damn weather.

The TV news people were always hyping up some tropical system or other, scaring people for the sake of ratings. He shook his head. The thing would probably blow itself out long before it made landfall, and even if it came ashore, the likelihood was it would veer off and go through Mississippi or the Florida Panhandle. As usual, the media were making a mountain out of a molehill. Now that they had a bear attack to go along with the storm, they must be over the moon.

He pushed the off button and watched the TV go dark, then pulled the trash bags from the two large waste containers behind the bar. They were full of bottles, old napkins, and discarded lemon slices. He heaved the two black bags over his shoulder and took them to the rear door, dropping them down ready to put into the dumpsters near the back fence. He was about to turn back toward the bar when a noise caught his attention.

It was nothing much, just a faint movement behind the metal paneled door, a scratching, shuffling sound.

He froze.

Ordinarily he would not have given the noise a second thought, but the news story stuck in his head. There was a wild animal on the loose. It could still be prowling around. Weren't bears attracted to trash?

He paused for a second, deciding what to do. He could leave the bags of garbage sitting inside until morning and go upstairs to bed, but then they would stink the place up to high heaven, not to mention the bugs it would attract. The health inspector could drop by anytime. He couldn't afford to encourage cockroaches. On the other hand, he didn't want to go outside if there was a dangerous animal lurking around. He wavered, unsure what to do. The thought of failing a health inspection won. He wasn't going outside unarmed, though. He hurried back to the bar and retrieved the baseball bat he kept hidden under the counter, relishing the heft and weight of the thing in his hand.

He returned to the back door and reached out to open it, then hesitated, overcome by a sudden sense of foreboding.

"Pull yourself together," he mumbled, although the words did little to ease his jangled nerves. Regardless, he reached out and pulled the handle, opening the door a crack and peering out.

The area behind the saloon comprised a paved access road skirted by a low fence. The dumpster stood next to the fence, one of its twin lids lifted to allow easy access. Beyond that, an open area ran down to a section of marshy grass, and then nothing but dark pine forest, the trees reaching fifty feet or more toward the sky, their thin trunks packed tight together.

He saw no sign of whatever had been moving around. He breathed a sigh of relief. There was no bear. He was alone.

He opened the door wide and stepped out, leaned the bat against the wall. He picked up the trash bags and walked to the dumpster, then hefted the first bag over the rim.

It fell inside with a dull thunk.

A menacing hiss rose from the dumpster's dark interior.

The hairs on the back of Ed's neck stood up. He felt a prickle of fear. There was something out here after all, and he'd been stupid enough to leave the bat all the way back at the bar's rear door.

He dropped the second bag and took and retreated, hoping whatever was in the dumpster stayed there. He'd barely moved a step before something large and black shot toward him, propelling itself out of the dumpster with unbelievable speed.

He screeched and stumbled away in a panic.

The creature lunged forward. The dumpster lid crashed closed behind it.

Ed's foot caught a crack in the concrete and he tumbled backward, his butt hitting the ground with a smack.

He let out a yelp of pain.

The beast landed a few feet away, a ball of hissing fur.

Ed laughed with relief. His assailant was nothing more than a large, fat raccoon. Two beady eyes studied him through patches of white and black fur. Then, without a sound, it turned and sauntered off back in the dumpster's direction before disappearing behind it.

He sat for a minute, feeling foolish, and then got to his feet. Thank goodness there was no one else around to see his humiliation at the hands of the raccoon.

He picked up the discarded bag of trash, lifted the dumpster lid, and threw the bag in, slamming the lid closed once more to foil the foraging animal should it try to get back inside.

He turned back toward the bar, collecting the baseball bat along the way. At the back door he stopped, looking for the furry pest, but saw no sign of the scavenger.

He was about to go back inside when he saw something else. Barely visible against the backdrop of the forest, hunched at the tree line, was an unfamiliar shape, large and muscular, with a tapered waist and stout, bulging legs.

Ed froze, surprised. An icy dread enveloped him.

The beast stood there, yellow eyes burning through the darkness.

Ed glanced down at the bat, his hands tightening on the grip until his knuckles turned white, ready for whatever might come next.

When he looked up again, the beast had vanished. He was alone. There was nothing lurking at the edge of the woods. All he saw were trees and darkness. He backed up, not wanting to be outside anymore. It was only after he closed the back door and ran the bolts across, that he felt safe again.

Chapter 25

TAYLOR CASSIDY RAN AS FAST as she could through the forest, weaving in and out of the trees, even though her legs felt like they were made of lead. Through the canopy of branches high above her, the reflected light of the moon cast dapple patterns across the ground, providing just enough light to see where she was going.

Somewhere to the rear she heard the beast crash through the foliage, grunting and growling as it went. It was close now, and gaining by the minute. She could not outrun the beast for much longer.

Ahead of her, through the tall pines, she saw the car sitting in a clearing. If only she could reach it she would be safe. But the car seemed so far away. She put on an extra spurt of speed, her body protesting the work, and sprinted forward.

She was almost there when her foot caught a root and sent her sprawling to the ground. She cried out as she landed; the force leaving her dazed and winded.

It was all the creature needed.

The beast closed the gap within seconds and then it was upon her, its body pressing her down, its mouth gaping to reveal rows of razor-sharp teeth. Foul breath assaulted her nose, causing her to wretch. The creature raised an arm. It slashed downward, sharp claws opening her throat from ear to ear...

~

TAYLOR SAT bolt upright in her bed.

Her eyes flew open.

A whimper escaped her mouth.

She looked around in a panic, heart pounding. For a moment the dream overlapped reality, but then it faded away and the familiar surroundings of her bedroom came into focus.

It was all a terrible dream. Nothing more. There was no monster ready to rip out her throat. The bedroom was silent and dark.

She took several deep breaths, willing her heart rate back to normal, then pushed the covers back and climbed out of bed. Her nightgown stuck to her, clammy and wet. A sheen of cold sweat covered her skin.

She padded to the bathroom and splashed water on her face, studying herself in the mirror for a moment. When she focused on the reflection of the room, she half expected to see the nightmare beast creeping toward her, its eyes glowing yellow, but the room was just the same as always.

She walked back to bed, pausing at the window on the way. Her eyes scanned the darkness of the woodland behind the house. Somewhere out there lurked the monster that killed Jake. That almost killed her.

She choked back a sob. Just yesterday everything was perfect, Jake was alive, and she was happy. Now it felt as if her world had ended.

She climbed back into bed and pulled the covers up, wishing there were more of the sleeping pills her mother had given her. She considered going to her mother's room, waking her and asking for some, since she was not sure she could sleep without them, but then the details of the nightmare came back, the monster chasing her, killing her. She did not want to risk another dream like that. Better to stay awake.

She glanced at the clock radio on the nightstand next to the bed. The red luminescent display said it was 3:15 a.m. It would be dawn in a couple of hours.

With any hope of going back to sleep abandoned, she padded to the closet and searched for her school yearbook. She pulled it out, returned to the bed, and flipped it through until she found what she was looking for. She touched a finger to the page, to the photo of Jake, his smiling face looking back at her. Then, despite her best efforts not to cry, the tears came once again.

Chapter 26

SHERIFF JOHN DECKER awoke as the first golden rays of dawn filled the bedroom. Next to him Nancy lay sprawled across the bed, the covers half off. He sat up and swung his legs off the bed.

"Good morning."

He glanced back to find Nancy smiling up at him. "Morning to you, too."

"Sneaking out in the middle of the night?"

"It's morning already. I have to meet Chad over on Route 16."

"Now?" Nancy rolled onto her back. "It's too early. Come back to bed."

"I'd love to," Decker said. "However, duty calls."

"Well, that stinks." Nancy grinned and beckoned to him. "Are you sure I can't persuade you?"

"You are making it very hard to leave. I can come back this evening though."

"I'd like that." Nancy smiled. "I should probably check on Taylor, anyway. I hope she's feeling better today."

"Give her some time. She's been though a lot."

"I know." Nancy bit her bottom lip. "Can I ask you something?"

"Sure." Decker shrugged.

"Why did you leave me here?"

"What do you mean?"

"You know what I mean. You left, I get that. Heaven knows, your father was hardly easy to live with. I get that. But why didn't you come back for me?"

"Nancy–"

"That night at prom, what we did, you were my first. I loved you. I gave myself to you."

"I can't change the past, Nancy."

"But you can give me an explanation. I waited months for you to come back for me. You never did."

"I was in a bad place back then."

"I need to know, John."

"Last night you said–"

"What happened last night was fun. I didn't need to know at that moment. I do now. I can't let myself fall for you again, not unless I can be sure you will stick around this time."

Decker returned to the bed and sat down. He reached out and took her hand. "I should have taken you with me, I know that now. I was young and stupid – I was afraid."

"There was no need to be."

"I'm back, that's what matters."

"Why did you come back?"

"I realized that what I'd run away to was no better than what I was running from."

"Something happened, didn't it?" Nancy said.

"My partner became involved in some bad stuff." Decker paused, thinking back to the last months in New York. "There was a crazy case. An ancient Egyptian statue and some bad people who wanted to take it. He helped them."

"He was on the take?"

"More like he sold out," Decker said. "He tried to kill me."

"John, I'm so sorry."

"Ancient history." He put his arm around her. "What matters is that I'm here, and I'm not going anywhere this time."

"Promise?"

"I promise." He pulled her close and kissed her. "I lost you once. I will not lose you again."

"Good," she murmured, pressing close to him.

"Maybe I can stay a few minutes longer," he said, slipping back beneath the sheets.

Chapter 27

WHEN DECKER ARRIVED at Route 16, Chad was already there, leaning against his cruiser with one foot up like a cowboy in an old western movie. Even though the sky was slate gray, the deputy still wore his Ray-Bans and wide-brimmed hat. Decker wondered if the man had watched too many 'Cops' reruns, imagining himself as the big hero, taking down the drunken wife beater as the guy tried to bolt half-dressed from the back door of some dilapidated trailer.

"Morning, boss," Chad said as Decker climbed from his vehicle.

"Morning." Decker reached into the back of the cruiser and retrieved his jacket.

"You look tired," Chad said.

"Didn't sleep too well last night," Decker replied, and it was true. It had been well into the early hours before he and Nancy had finished making love, not to mention their brief liaison this morning, but that wasn't the only reason he had gotten little sleep. Images of Jake, his body ripped open and torn, haunted his dreams.

"Me either," Chad said. "Couldn't stop thinking about that poor kid."

"Yeah." Decker didn't want to dwell on it anymore. He would rather think of happier things, like Nancy, and the way she felt as he held her in his arms and made love to her.

"You want a doughnut?" Chad stuck his head into the car and came out with a brown bag. "They're fresh." He opened the bag and pulled out a ring of fried dough, examining it. "At least they were yesterday when I bought them."

"No. Thanks."

"Suit yourself." Chad bit into the doughnut and chewed loudly. "So what's the plan?"

"I have a feeling our missing moonshiner didn't just abandon his truck and decide to hide out in the woods. Apparently he was with Terry Boudreaux, who is also missing."

"And you figure that since we found that claw the same thing that got Jake might have gotten them too." Chad popped the last of the doughnut into his mouth and chewed loudly.

"Maybe. It's just a hunch, but if so there should be some evidence of it up here somewhere."

"Question is, where?" Chad motioned toward the woods. "There must be thousands of acres of woodland all around us. How in the hell are we going to find them?"

"With a whole lot of luck," Decker said. "But if I'm right, they won't be too far from the road. Whatever killed Jake left him where he was. It didn't drag him off or try to bury him for later. Maybe it did the same with Floyd and Terry."

"Boy, that's a long shot. We don't even know what got to Jake, let alone its habits."

"It's all we've got to go on," Decker said. "I figure we'll split up. You take one side of the road, and I'll take the other. We'll search an area for a hundred yards in each direction from the spot where the truck was, and two hundred yards back into the woods."

"Great." Chad did not look pleased at splitting up.

"Holler if you find anything." Decker opened the trunk of the cruiser and pulled out the shotguns. He offered one to the deputy. "Better take this."

"If you hear me fire this, you'd better come running."

Chad took the gun and hitched it over his shoulder. "Same here."

"I'll take the left side." He walked off toward the woods.

Decker watched him depart and then headed in the other direction. He stepped from the blacktop onto the verge and into the woods.

Once he was under the forest canopy, Decker wished he hadn't suggested they split up. The woods felt oppressive, claustrophobic and eerie.

He lifted the shotgun and made sure that the safety was off, and then moved forward at a snail's pace, keeping the gun high lest he come across anything unexpected. He proceeded at a slow pace, searching every inch of ground, but saw nothing out of place.

He pushed onward, weaving around fallen branches and tree trunks, stopping every few minutes to take stock of his surroundings. As he went, he kept a careful eye on the ground to make sure he was not stepping anywhere that he shouldn't. The last thing he wanted was to get bitten by a coral snake.

When he reached the furthest point of the search area, he turned and moved back along the same line, but further in. Still, there was nothing. He was about to turn again and complete another leg, when the sound of Chad's voice, faint but unmistakable, carried on the breeze.

Decker picked his way back to the road and crossed over, entering the woods on the other side. It didn't take him long to find the deputy.

"I think I've found something," Chad said, motioning toward something small and black on the ground a few yards ahead.

Decker bent down and examined it, realizing with a jolt he

was looking at a man's shoe, complete with the foot still in it. A bloody stump left little clue to the whereabouts of the owner. "Dammit," Decker mumbled. He'd hoped he was wrong about the moonshiners. "Let's keep going."

"You don't want to call for backup?" Chad asked.

"What backup?" Decker raised an eyebrow. "We're the only two cops in the entire town."

"I know." Chad looked disappointed. "I was just hoping you might bring in the Staties."

"Hell no," Decker said as they ambled forward. "State troopers? You don't think we can handle this ourselves?"

"Maybe not." Chad froze, pointing.

Decker followed his gaze. The sight before them made him thankful he hadn't bothered with that doughnut. Sprawled on the ground between two large pines was Terry Boudreaux, a silent scream etched on his face. Something had ripped his neck open, leaving it a bloody mess. Below that, his body was a jumbled chaos of raw bone and guts.

Decker skirted the corpse. The cloying, sickly sweet odor of decay hung in the air and he fought the urge to gag. Flies buzzed around the remains. Decker swatted at the closest insects, shuddering as they landed on his arms and face. Chad followed up the rear, almost bumping into the sheriff in his haste to move past the mutilated cadaver.

A few yards to the right they found the abandoned truck's other occupant, his back against a pine trunk.

Floyd Benson looked up at them with a dead stare, his insides spilling onto the soft earth.

Chad turned to Decker, his face ashen. "That clears one thing up. It wasn't rival moonshiners. Unless they had a pack of rabid dogs, that is."

Chapter 28

ED JOHNSON WOKE in the dim light of his upstairs room above the County Line Saloon. He rolled over and laid on his back, where he stayed for several minutes, unwilling to move, his mind still half submerged in sleep. His thoughts turned to the night before, and the shape watching from the edge of the forest. It was not a bear. That much he knew. In fact, it reminded him of something that happened years before, when he was just a kid playing out in the pine woods behind his grandmother's house.

∿

IT WAS the summer of 1975. He was walking back from a stream that meandered past the property, fishing pole over his shoulder, a couple of catfish in a bucket. It was a glorious summer day, with blue skies and a gentle breeze that took the edge off the stifling Southern Louisiana heat. He listened to the birds in the branches high above as they called to each other and sang. He watched squirrels play, hopping from tree to tree and scurrying around, all the while chattering in excitement.

And then, in an instant, everything changed.

A silence fell over the forest. The birds stopped singing. The crickets ceased their chirping. Even the sun slipped behind a cloud.

At first he noticed nothing amiss and kept on walking, oblivious to all but the pail of fish that would cook up great for supper.

Until a twig snapped. It was little more than a single sharp crack, but it filled the void and focused him upon the surreal silence of his surroundings.

He stopped and stood still, his ten-year-old heart pounding in his chest. A crawling sense of unease enveloped him.

Something moved off to Ed's left.

He turned to look. As his eyes adjusted to the gloom between the trees and he saw something he would never forget.

A beast unlike any he had ever seen. It stood occupying the space between two tall pines, an arm holding on to each, claws gripping the tree trunks.

It studied him with hooded eyes that burned yellow as sulfur.

Ed dropped the bucket of fish. He knew he should run, but his legs refused to move.

The creature took a step forward.

Ed found his legs. He let out a scream, a shriek that reached notes high enough to make a choirmaster dance with joy, and took off through the woods.

He ran at a breakneck pace, ignoring the branches and thorns that tore at his skin and bloodied his arms and legs.

He didn't stop until he reached the familiar surroundings of his grandmother's yard. Only then did he chance looking back toward the trees, but there was nothing there. He was alone.

He reached the house, taking the porch steps two at a time. He fell through the door and slammed it behind him. Only then did he take a moment to catch his breath, leaning over, sweat dripping from his face onto the polished wood floor.

"What on earth has gotten into you?" His grandmother asked, poking her head from the kitchen. There was a smudge of flour on her forehead.

"I saw a monster in the woods. It chased me."

"What's that, child?" His grandmother set her rolling pin on the counter and focused her attention on him. "Now, why would you think a monster was chasing you?"

"I saw it. I swear." Ed was crying now, large tears that rolled down his cheeks and lingered on his chin. "It was standing there, looking at me. I think..." He gulped between sobs. "I think it wanted to eat me."

"My Lord. Calm down before you have a fit," the old woman said. "Tell me what you saw. Quickly now."

"It was a monster." Ed gulped. "It had yellow eyes and looked like a big dog, only on two legs, and it had huge claws and teeth..."

"I see." His grandmother kneeled down and took him by the shoulders. "Now you listen to me boy, you're not to tell anyone about this, do you hear?"

Ed nodded. "Why not?"

"Because people won't believe you. They will say that you didn't see it."

"But I saw it."

"I know you did, child. I know what you saw." She stood and shuffled back to the kitchen. "You had better stay out of the woods from now on."

"I will." He meant it too. He had no intention of ever stepping foot in those woods again. "What was it, Grammy?"

The old woman turned and looked at him, her face stern. "It was the devil, boy. A beast dragged from the pits of hell to make the heathens and the fornicators pay for their sins." She waved a bony finger at him. "You just crossed paths with the Loup-Garou."

ED HAD PUT this incident from his mind for decades, blocked it out and pretended it was the imagination of a small child, fueled by the mad ramblings of a superstitious woman who still believed the old legends.

But now he knew better. The Loup-Garou found him that hot summer day, and last night it came back.

Chapter 29

IT WAS early afternoon before Sheriff Decker slipped away from the grisly scene in the woods off Route 16. He sent Chad to the Boudreaux house to talk to Jeremiah, and drove back to town, leaving the M.E., with whom he had spent far too much time over the past 24 hours, examining the victims.

He made it through the door of the sheriff's Office just in time to avoid the first drops of rain that fell from the swiftly darkening sky.

Waiting there, propped up against the front counter, with a look on his face that could sink a ship, was Mayor Thornton.

"What can I do for you, Beau?" Decker put on his cheeriest face.

"Sheriff Decker. How are you?" The mayor did little to hide the annoyance in his voice.

"Well, I've had better days, to tell the truth, Beau."

"Really. Me too. You know, I was getting ready for bed last night, when I saw a rather interesting news item on Channel 36. You wouldn't know what that was all about, would you?"

Decker walked behind the counter and stopped at the coffeepot. He poured himself a cup and took a sip. "Not sure I follow," he said, knowing full well what Thornton referred to.

"Oh, I think you do. How else would the local news have found out about the killing up at Sullivan's Pond yesterday?"

"Ah. That."

"Yes, that." Mayor Thornton took a step forward. "I would truly love an explanation."

"I beg your pardon?" Decker felt his ire rising. The mayor may be in charge of the town at large. But Decker was the sheriff, at liberty to protect the public by whatever means he saw fit.

"You had no right to leak information about Jake Barlow's death to the media."

"I didn't leak anything," Decker replied through gritted teeth. "I issued an official statement."

"If I didn't agree to it, the statement was not official." Beau folded his arms and glared at Decker. "I decide what the townsfolk are told, and what they are not. The last thing we need is a panic over nothing. The elections are coming up in the Fall. We need to handle situations like this with sensitivity."

"A panic over nothing?" Decker said. He couldn't help noticing the muscle at the corner of Thornton's eye twitching. The man did not like his authority being usurped. "Mayor, there is a dangerous animal on the loose. If you think I give a rat's ass about you winning reelection, then you are sadly mistaken."

"Might I remind you, Sheriff, your own job is also up for reelection."

"And if the good people of Wolf Haven choose someone else in November, then good for them, but in the meantime I am going to do my job as I see fit, and right now that means warning the town about whatever killed those three people."

"Three?"

"Yes. Three." Decker relished the look of shock on the Mayor's face. "We found two more bodies this morning. Floyd Benson and Terry Boudreaux."

"Floyd Benson, the moonshiner?"

"The very same." He almost asked the Mayor how many other Floyd Benson's he knew, but thought better of it.

"Good riddance." Thornton shook his head. "The man was nothing but trouble."

"That's all very well, but it's not just going after malcontents and petty criminals. People might not give a hoot about some old moonshiner, but they sure as hell don't want their kids getting ripped up." Decker rubbed a spot above his temple where a dull pain throbbed. The start of a tension headache.

"Regardless, you should have cleared it with me first."

"Maybe. Too late now, though. It's already done," Decker said, evenly.

"A word of advice." The Mayor lowered his voice. "Don't make the mistake of getting too close to this thing John, too involved."

"I'm not too close." Decker knew where this was going.

The Mayor was not finished. "I know this must be hard for you, what with the way your mother died, but this isn't the same situation."

"I never said it was," replied Decker. "Still, now you mention it, there are certain similarities."

"Coincidence, Sheriff. Nothing more. Don't throw your job away by following in your father's footsteps."

"Thanks for the sage advice," Decker said. If the Mayor was looking to annoy him it was working. "If you don't mind, I have a lot to do. I need to hunt down whatever is running around out there and kill it."

"Well, for heaven's sake, do so quietly and do it quickly. When that new interstate spur goes in I want people to use it. We need folk to come here and spend their hard-earned dollars. They won't do that if they believe they might get eaten." He stomped toward the door and slammed it on his way out.

"Whatever you say, Mayor." Decker murmured, although the Mayor was no longer around to hear it. Then for good measure, he added, "asshole."

Carol, who had been silent during the entire exchange, finally spoke. "What kind of bug got up his ass?"

"Who knows?" Decker poured a second coffee. "Did you get in touch with anyone who can help us with that claw?"

"I did." She rummaged through the pages of her notebook. "I spoke with one Professor Juliette Costa over at LSU in Baton Rouge. She was very interested and asked me to email her a couple of photographs of the claw. I did as she requested first thing this morning."

"And?" Decker hoped it was good news. If they could identify the killer, they could trap it, or even kill it.

"She got back to me about an hour ago. Whatever this thing is, it didn't come from a bear. It also doesn't fit an alligator."

"So what did it come from?"

"That's just it. She doesn't know. It's like nothing she has ever seen before. We can have the claw sent over to her for DNA testing, but she couldn't make a visual identification."

"That's not much help. You'd better package it up and overnight it to her. The quicker we identify this thing, the better."

"Already done. The parcel is waiting for pickup as we speak."

"Did she say how long it would take?" Decker knew that labs could take weeks to return results.

"A few days. Week at most. She's going to fast track it, given our circumstances."

"Did she give us anything to go on in the meantime?" Decker asked. "Has she ever come across a situation like this before?"

"Not that she mentioned. Apart from bears, which themselves are very rare, there are no other large predatory mammals indigenous to this part of the country, at least, not ones that have claws like this. It might be an invasive species, or something kept as a pet that escaped." Carol did not look convinced.

Neither was Decker. "I'd hate to meet the pet that could do this." He wondered if he should follow Chad's advice and bring in someone better equipped to deal with the situation. Trouble was, he had no clue who that would be. Animal attacks didn't really fall under the auspices of the State Police, and the Louisiana Department of Wildlife and Fisheries were more concerned with illegal hunting than trapping dangerous animals. It looked like they were on their own, at least for now.

"There's one more thing." Carol looked uneasy, as if she didn't want to be the bearer of bad news.

"Go on. Let's hear it," Decker sighed. He remembered the Mayor's words. Not being reelected as sheriff was looking more and more appealing by the minute.

"There's a tropical storm brewing out in The Gulf. It's still a few days away, and might not even head our way, but right now we're as likely to get it as anyone."

"Fantastic." Decker put the cup down and rubbed his neck to relieve a knot of tension that throbbed at the base of his skull. "Bad weather. That's all we need."

Chapter 30

JEREMIAH BOUDREAUX LISTENED to Chad in stunned silence, the remains of a ferocious hangover pounding inside his head. He hadn't let the deputy inside, opting instead to leave him on the stoop. This was partly out of principle, but also because he couldn't remember if he had anything less than legal lying around the house. He was pretty sure there was some weed in the bedroom, and one look at the hooch bottle would be a giveaway he didn't get it at the liquor store. Also, the flat screen TV in the living room would probably not hold up to more than a cursory examination. He hadn't exactly acquired it through the usual channels.

None of that mattered now.

Terry was dead.

The words seemed unreal, as if they didn't belong together in the same sentence. He wondered if he was still sleeping, and this was nothing more than an alcohol-fueled fabrication of his booze-soaked mind. He wished it were. He prayed he would wake up on the old worn out sofa, a liquor bottle in his hand and Terry standing over him scowling because he'd drank all the liquor without sharing. But he would not wake up, he knew, because this was no dream. His son was gone.

He slumped against the doorframe. Everything felt out of whack, like he was watching the scene as a detached observer. He felt numb. "How did it happen?" His voice sounded oddly feeble and small.

"It appears a wild animal attacked him."

"That isn't possible," Jeremiah said. "How could it be an animal?"

"I don't know, sir." Chad dropped his eyes. He fidgeted with his sunglasses, passing them from hand to hand. "We haven't identified the culprit yet."

"Did it get Floyd too?" Jeremiah hoped it had, because if the old bastard somehow escaped, Jeremiah would finish the job. "Is Floyd dead?"

"Yes, sir. He surely is." Chad nodded. Jeremiah thought he saw a look of sympathy pass across the young man's face.

"Good." Jeremiah felt a flicker of satisfaction among the grief. "That man was bad for my Terry." His throat tightened. He felt wetness at the corners of his eyes. "Are you absolutely sure my son is dead?"

"Yes, sir. Quite sure."

"You saw it for yourself?"

"I did. There's no doubt," the deputy said, his voice low.

"Where is he now?" Jeremiah turned to pick up his coat. "Take me to him."

"I, uh…" Chad searched for words. "I don't think that would be for the best, at least not right now. There might have to be a formal identification, but…"

"I want to see my boy." Jeremiah felt the tears streaming down his face, and for the first time in his life, he did not care. "Dammit man, I need to see Terry."

"I'll have to run it by the sheriff. To be honest with you, Terry was not in good shape when we found him. You, uh…"

Chad paused and took a deep breath. "You might not want to remember him like that."

"You talk to Decker." Jeremiah raised himself up, a bitter anger fighting the grief for control of his emotions. "I want to see Terry. And I will, one way or the other. Even if I have to kick down a door."

"I'll talk to the sheriff and see what I can do. I can't promise anything though." Chad pulled a card from his breast pocket and offered it to Jeremiah. "In the meantime, I would suggest you stay out of the woods, and call us if you need anything." Chad hovered for a second, as if he wanted to say something more, but then he turned and walked back to the cruiser.

Jeremiah watched him pull away and recede down the dirt road amid a cloud of dust. He looked down at the card, at the number for the Sheriff's Office printed upon it. He crumpled the card and threw it to the ground, then he picked up the empty hooch bottle and threw it against the wall with a mighty scream.

Chapter 31

IT WAS GETTING dark when John Decker entered the County Line Saloon and made straight for the bar. The room was gloomy. A faint smell of stale beer hung in the air. Decker glanced around, taking in the worn tables and booths, and the faded posters clinging to the walls in gold-rimmed frames. Two Pinball machines stood in a nook near the bar. Only one was on, its lights flashing in random patterns to entice players. On the other, taped to the glass, was a tattered Out-of-Order sign. The place had seen better days for sure, but it was Wolf Haven's lone drinking establishment, and Decker needed a drink.

When he approached the bar, Ed eyed him with caution.

"Evening, sheriff. Can I help you?"

"A cold beer would be nice." Decker took a barstool and looked around, noting the lack of customers.

"Sure thing." Ed took a glass from a shelf behind the bar and then turned back to Decker. "Tough day, huh?"

"Something like that." Decker watched the bartender pour his drink and place it on the bar top.

"I hear you found Floyd and his sidekick up in the woods, ripped up just like the Barlow kid."

"Word travels fast." Decker took his beer and sipped it.

"It's a small town. People talk."

"Apparently."

Ed paused for a moment, as if weighing up what to say next, then spoke again, his voice low. "Listen, Sheriff, there's something I need to tell you."

Decker looked up from his beer.

Ed rested his elbows on the bar, leaning close to Decker. "I know what killed them."

"Really?" Decker put his drink down. "And you didn't think to share that information?"

"I'm telling you now, aren't I?"

"Alright, you have my attention."

"I saw the killer." Ed took a deep breath. "It was here last night, out behind the bar, just standing at the edge of the woods watching me. Creepy as hell I can tell you."

"What was watching you Ed, a bear?"

"This was no bear. It was something else, and it was big, real big. And its eyes, burning yellow…"

Decker sat up. Taylor had mentioned the same thing, yellow eyes. "Go on."

"It stood there, looking at me like it was trying to figure out what to do. I reached for my bat, but when I looked back, it had disappeared. Scared the shit out of me. I got back inside real quick, I can tell you." Ed took a deep breath. "Thing is, this isn't the first time I've seen it. I know you will think I'm crazy, but I saw the same beast when I was a kid. Out in the woods behind my grandmother's house."

"That's impossible."

"I know what I saw last night, and I know what I saw back then."

"So where's it been hiding for the last three decades?" Decker raised an eyebrow. "Whatever you think you saw when you were a kid, it isn't the same animal that's killing people now. It can't be."

"You of all people should take this seriously. It killed your own mother all those years ago."

"Now hang on—"

Ed interrupted him. "Your mother died around the same time I saw the beast in the woods years ago, and then last night I saw it again, and now the killings are starting all over again. We have a problem in this town, Sheriff. Something has come back, something bad."

"Nothing has come back." Decker fixed the bartender with an icy stare, barely controlling the anger that simmered below the surface. "My mother's death was an accident, nothing more."

"Think what you will, Sheriff, but I know what's out there. It's the Loup-Garou, seeking revenge on those that have crossed it."

"The what?" Decker stared at the bartender in disbelief. "Come on, Ed, that's crazy talk."

"Someone summoned the spirit of the Loup-Garou, Sheriff. It's here among us, and it'll keep killing until it gets what it wants."

"The Loup-Garou?" Decker asked, incredulous.

"A person who can summon the spirit of the wolf and change into the beast at will. Forget all that crap about full moons, this thing will come for you day or night, a living nightmare with one thing on its mind. Killing."

"I know the legend of the Loup-Garou. It's a fairy tale, nothing more."

"I wouldn't be so quick to rule it out if I were you."

"This is ridiculous. I've got better things to do than listen to unfounded superstitions," Decker said. "And you need to keep your mouth shut. The town's scared enough without you dragging up old myths of werewolves, spreading fear and panic for no reason."

"It's no myth, Sheriff, you'll see." Ed shook his head. "You'd better watch your back. It could be anyone."

"I think I've had just about enough crazy talk for one night." Decker pushed the beer away and dropped a five-dollar bill on the bar. "Keep the change." He stood and walked to the door, then stepped out into the night. Whatever was running around Wolf Haven was flesh and blood, not some mythical creature created to frighten children into behaving.

Chapter 32

BENNY TOWNSEND, owner of the Pump and Go gas station, was fast asleep on his sofa, a half-empty can of beer fighting gravity to stay upright in his hand. He was dreaming of his high school girlfriend, Janna. They were behind the bleachers fooling around, something that hadn't happened in real life, much to his chagrin. He was about to slip his hand inside her blouse, finally cop a feel, when a loud crash jolted him from the fantasy.

His eyes flew open.

He wondered what had roused him from his slumber. If someone had pulled into the gas station, the bell, triggered by a sensor near the pump, would have rung, but whatever had woken him was not a customer wanting to fill up.

He listened for a moment but heard nothing. Whatever had disturbed him, everything was quiet now. Maybe he'd imagined the noise, dreamed it.

He was about to close his eyes and drift back to sleep when a second crash broke the silence.

This time there was no mistaking it. He jumped up and ran to the window. He pulled the curtain back and peered out, but there was only darkness beyond the double-wide trailer standing behind the station's convenience store.

He felt a pang of disappointment. The dream was fading, returning to the ether whence it came. He wouldn't get to see what happened with Janna. He clung to the vague snatches that remained until they too gave way to reality.

He made his way to the door, his hand resting on the knob. It was late, and there shouldn't be anyone around. A shiver raced up his spine. What if delinquents were breaking into the gas station intent on vandalism, or worse? Only last month, in the dead of night, someone had cut the rubber hoses that connected the pumps to the nozzles. It had cost him a thousand bucks to replace them. It also put the gas pumps out of commission for two days, which meant a bunch of lost sales. Not his time.

He reached out and flipped the deadlock, pulled the door open, and stepped out into the cool night air.

A motion activated security light snapped on, illuminating the space between the battered double wide and the gas station. A tow truck stood idle between the structures, its dull metal hook hanging like a strange medieval torture device. Beyond that, several rusting oil barrels stood stacked one atop the other next to a pile of flattened shipping boxes that once contained candy bars, toilet paper and other convenience store items.

Benny crept forward, his eyes darting left to right, searching for whatever caused the sounds that woke him, but nothing looked out of place.

He reached the tow truck and skirted it, crossing to the building that housed the convenience store, hugging the wall of the building as he approached the forecourt.

Four gas pumps came into view, sheltered under a steel frame awning that leaned slightly to the left, thanks to a slightly inebriated driver a couple years back. He kept meaning to fix it, but somehow never found the time. Besides, it hadn't come tumbling down yet, so he figured it was still structurally sound.

Benny took a step toward the pumps. When he saw the reason for the two loud crashes, he stopped dead in his tracks.

Next to the front door of the shop stood a cage that housed propane gas bottles for grills and campers. One side held empty canisters, while the other side held full bottles.

Except that neither side contained much of anything now.

The metal grill that secured the bottles was twisted and bent, hanging free except for one buckled hinge. Littered across the pavement in front of the cage were the gas canisters, some standing upright as if carefully placed on the ground. Others lay on their side, rocking gently in the night breeze. Some canisters sported dents.

"Shit." Benny grimaced. As if money wasn't tight enough, now he would have to replace the canisters. Running a gas station was not the lucrative venture it once was, thanks to state and federal taxation and slim profit margins. Being in a small town like Wolf Haven didn't help either.

He retrieved a canister and hoisted it back into the storage cage, then lifted another. He was about to pick up a third when he stopped, the hairs on the back of his neck standing straight. A feeling of foreboding came upon him. Even though he had heard nothing, had seen nothing, he knew instinctively that he was not alone. The air felt heavy, oppressive. The frogs that usually croaked at night had fallen silent. Even the crickets had stopped their chirping.

Benny stood still. He scanned the station's forecourt and the empty road beyond.

And then he saw it.

The creature crouched between two pumps. Sitting motionless on its haunches, it watched him with yellow eyes. Then, before Benny could comprehend what he was looking at, it lunged toward him.

Chapter 33

AFTER HE LEFT THE BAR, Decker made his way down Main Street toward Cassidy's Diner. As he walked, he did his best to push Ed Johnson's ramblings from his mind. There were better things to think of, like Nancy, and their reignited relationship. By the time he reached Cassidy's, he'd all but forgotten the strange conversation in the County Line.

The Diner was dark and closed, a handwritten sign taped to the door announcing the restaurant would reopen the following week. Decker walked past and up the narrow access road to the house. He rang the doorbell.

Nancy answered. She smiled when she saw him, but behind the gesture Decker sensed a weary sadness.

"I was hoping it was you," She held the door open for Decker to enter.

"How is she?" He looked past Nancy toward the living room, where a TV played. "Taylor?"

"She's been better. The doctor prescribed sedatives. She's upstairs sleeping right now."

"How are you coping?" Decker reached out and took her hand.

"It's hard." Nancy steered him toward the living room and

picked up the remote, then turned off the TV. "Better now that you are here." She put her arms around Decker, kissed him, and nuzzled into his chest, her head on his shoulder.

Decker held her close, not sure what to say next, but happy to be there with her.

It was while they were standing there in each other's arms that Decker's radio squawked.

He went outside before responding, not wanting to disturb Taylor. Nancy stood in the doorway, watching with concern on her face.

After he finished with the dispatcher, Decker turned to Nancy. "I'm so sorry. There's been an incident. I need to deal with this."

"Go," she said. "Take care of it. I'll be fine here."

"Stay inside and lock the door." Decker instructed her. "Don't go anywhere. Don't let anyone in."

"I won't." Nancy reached out and grabbed his arm. "Come back later? I'll feel safer if you're here."

"I will," Decker said. "I'll come back. I promise."

He descended Nancy's steps and hurried along Main Street. As he walked, it began to rain. By the time he reached the sheriff's Office, the rain had turned into a downpour and the afternoon was dark as night. He made a beeline for his cruiser and jumped in, flicked on the windshield wipers, and pulled out onto Main. He activated the siren and light bar, the eerie blue and red strobes dancing across the buildings on both sides of the street. The town felt eerily deserted as he sped toward the Pump and Go. It was like people already knew there was danger lurking beyond their four walls, and were huddling inside, afraid it might come for them next. Decker felt it too. Evil was visiting Wolf Haven. A malevolent force that wanted nothing more than to cause death and terror. He only hoped he could stop it.

Chapter 34

TAYLOR CASSIDY STOOD at her bedroom window and watched the sheriff leave. She should have been sleeping, and for a few hours she had dozed off, thanks to the sedatives the doctor gave her.

As it had done many times over the past twenty-four hours, her mind wandered to Jake and the beast in the woods. It was still out there, and it wanted to finish what it started. It wanted her. She didn't really understand how she knew this. Maybe it was the way the beast looked at her through the car window as she frantically tried to start the engine and pull away, as though it recognized her. That was a crazy thought. It was an animal, nothing more. At least, that's what she told herself.

It started to rain. Huge globs of water that dropped from the dark and angry storm clouds gathering over Wolf Haven. The downpour created a rhythmic tapping sound, like a thousand drumming fingers. It was fitting the weather had turned bad. It was as if the skies were reflecting the mood of the town. Or maybe it was a harbinger of something worse yet to come. She hoped not, but she could not shake the nagging feeling that neither she nor the town had not seen the end of the bloodshed.

She turned away from the window and picked up her cell phone. She tapped the unlock code and opened up the text messages, browsed to the last conversation with Jake. As she read the words, a sob caught in her throat.

If only she had not suggested going up to that stupid swimming hole. If they had gone bowling like Jake suggested, he would still be alive. It was her fault Jake was dead, and all because she wanted to fool around. She wished she could send him one last message, send it back in time to yesterday and tell him to stay home where it was safe. Her fingers hovered over the keyboard, and then she typed, picking out a last message to her boyfriend. She paused a moment and then hit send. The message appeared in a blue box under the other ones.

'I love you.'

Then she dropped the phone into her lap and cried.

Chapter 35

WHEN DECKER ARRIVED at the Pump and Go it was already a hive of activity. Two cruisers blocked the road. One was Chad's vehicle. The other was a white Chevy Tahoe with State Police emblazoned along the side. An ambulance idled nearby, back doors open. The gas station was ringed with crime scene tape. Silhouetted figures moved across the forecourt, lit occasionally by the pop of a camera flash.

Decker pulled his car behind the State Police vehicle and climbed out, ducking under the tape and making his way toward the cluster of uniforms standing under the canopy near the pumps.

Chad turned to him, a grim look upon his face. "We have another one. Just like the others."

As Decker approached, one of the State officers, a sergeant according to the three chevrons on his arm, edged sideways to let him through. Despite mentally preparing himself, Decker flinched when he saw the body.

Benny Townsend had seen better days. He lay sliced open, his guts splashed across the concrete. A slick film of rain coated his skin and drenched his clothing, washing blood off him in crimson rivulets toward the storm drain grate a few feet away. He lay with his arms and legs spread wide, as if he'd just lay down to take a nap right there amid the gas pumps, except that he was missing a fair proportion of his stomach and groin area. Something had made quick work of dispatching him with a ferociousness that left Decker feeling queasy. He looked away and took several deep breaths, trying to ignore the stench of death that wafted from the mutilated corpse. Finally, his composure returned. "Who found the victim?"

"Over there." Chad pointed to a young woman sitting on the rear platform of the ambulance. Wrapped in a gray blanket, she hugged herself as if cold despite the humidity. "She found the victim when she stopped for gas."

The State officer with the stripes on his arm spoke up. "We heard the call over the radio. We were close by and responded."

"Has anyone spoken with her yet?" Decker asked.

"Only briefly. She was hysterical, so the medic administered a sedative to calm her down." Chad said.

"I want a statement as soon as she's up to it."

Chad nodded.

"Not that there's any doubt what did this." Decker glanced back toward the corpse and instantly regretted it. The bile rose in his throat and he fought to keep himself from throwing up. The last thing he wanted to do was contaminate the scene with the remains of his lunch. He stepped away and took a deep breath. To his relief, the nausea subsided.

"You alright, boss?" Chad was watching him with a look of concern on his face.

"I'm fine," Decker said. "Just a little tired."

Chad nodded and turned back to the crime scene.

Decker rubbed his temples. A dull ache throbbed behind his eyes. He would take an Aspirin as soon as he got back to the car. Christ, this was turning into a shitty week.

Chapter 36

ANNIE DOUCET LEANED BACK on the small cot in the corner of her one-room shack and rested her head on the pillow. She felt weary to the bone.

The cabin was dark and quiet, save for the flickering red light cast by the fire within the potbelly stove, and the occasional crackle of burning wood. The room was hot, but Annie, as usual, was cold. Not even the warmth from the stove did much to take the edge off her chill.

She closed her eyes, her thoughts turning, as they had so many times over the past few weeks, to the new road the town wanted to put in. It seemed like a futile effort to her. Wolf Haven had survived for more than a hundred years without the road, and it would survive just fine without it now. No, it was pure greed that motivated the Mayor and his lap dogs to build that infernal highway and steal her land. Who cared if the road would bring more business to town? There were more important things than money. Not that Nancy Cassidy, Ed Johnson, and the other members of the local Chamber of Commerce saw it that way. All they wanted to do was line their own pockets with gold. Just like that bastard, Floyd Benson, agreeing to hand over his land like that, taking their dirty money. Not that it would do him much good now, lying on some mortician's table. Same thing went for the Barlows. They wouldn't be attending any Chamber meetings for a while with their son, Jake, all chewed up and dead. It seemed only fair that they lose something they loved. They were taking everything from Annie without even a second thought. That Cassidy kid, Taylor, was still around though. She'd had a lucky escape, and that was a shame. Spoiled bitch. Still, her time would come. How did the saying go? You reap what you sow? Pretty soon Mayor Beau Thornton and all the other folk who conspired to take her home would get theirs. Of that, she was sure.

A flash of lightning lit the room, throwing the cramped space into stark relief and casting brief shadows across the floor. Behind this came a low rumble of thunder. The weather was deteriorating by the hour. Soon a mighty maelstrom would descend upon the small town of Wolf Haven, but that didn't matter to Annie. There were worse things than a storm, as the town would find out soon enough.

She opened her eyes and glanced toward the window, and the lashing rain that hammered upon it. Maybe in a while she would go out. Enjoy the night. But first she needed to rest.

Chapter 37

IT WAS LATE by the time Decker pulled away from the Pump and Go gas station. The scene shrank away in his rearview mirror until all he could see were faint pulses of blue and red in the darkness. The strobes atop the emergency vehicles still present. Soon these too faded into the inky blackness. He felt dog-tired and more than a little disturbed.

He drove back to Nancy's house in a daze. The rain, which fell in a downpour so hard his wipers could barely clear it from his windshield, did little to improve his mood. A few days ago this had been a peaceful place, a great place to live, a great place to heal.

It still sometimes felt strange that he was back here, in Wolf Haven. A long time ago he'd run away, ran far from this place, from his father's obsessions and bouts of temper, but trouble followed like a constant companion. It hid at first, lurked in the background, but then his partner, a man Decker trusted, sold him out and tried to kill him. Turning his friend in had been hard, almost dying at the hands of that same friend, even harder. And so he came back to Wolf Haven, a place where nothing ever happened, where the jail went weeks at a time with no one in it. This was a place from another time

when people still left their doors unlocked at night and neigh-
bors looked out for one other. No one would leave their door
unlocked tonight, though.

As he drove, he scanned the road ahead, his eyes drifting
to the dark woods on either side of the vehicle. He wasn't sure
what he was looking for, but somewhere out there was a
monster. Something powerful and angry enough to inflict the
carnage he saw at the Pump and Go. Even as he concentrated
on driving, he could still see the body of Benny Townsend, his
arms and legs spread wide, the rest of him nothing more than
a mass of torn flesh and bone. It sickened him.

His thoughts turned to Nancy. She was the one good thing
in all of this, an angel that had come into his life when he least
expected it, and for that he was glad. Heaven knows she had
enough reasons not to get involved with him, especially after
the way he'd treated her all those years ago.

None of that mattered right now. She was vulnerable. She
needed him as much as he needed her. He wondered if either
of them could cope with what was happening if it weren't for
the other.

He was still musing on this when he reached the town, his
patrol car moving down Main Street at a snail's pace. It would
be good for people to see that he was there if they needed
him. Not that there was a sign of anyone. Word had gotten
around about the attacks, and the entire town had locked
themselves in their homes for the night. Even the County Line
Saloon was empty, with only a pair of cars parked out front,
and he knew one of those was Ed's own vehicle.

The town was on a self-imposed lockdown.

He knew how they felt. Fear of the unknown was a
powerful force. During the months after his mother's death, he
was sure something was coming for him too. He lay awake at
night, cowering under the covers, waiting for the bogeyman to
arrive, while down below, on the first floor, his father grew
ever more obsessed with finding her killer. The bogeyman

never came, and his father never found the peace he needed. Instead, he filled boxes with police reports and crazy theories. If the old man were still alive, these latest killings would surely spark a renewed bout of obsession. They could not be related, of course. That much Decker was sure of. But he could not ignore the similarities. It surely wasn't the same animal, but it could be a descendant, the offspring of whatever beast perpetrated that horrendous act so long ago. If that were the case, maybe there was something in those old notebooks and files he could use. Even though he had no desire to dredge up a past he'd spent too long trying to forget, Decker knew what he must do. He swung the cruiser around and drove away from Nancy's, and back toward his own house.

Chapter 38

NANCY CASSIDY SAT on the sofa with the TV on low in the background and a cup of cocoa on the coffee table in front of her. On the screen a TV reporter rehashed the events of the past few days, describing the recent killings with zeal probably better reserved for covering the church Fete, or July fourth festivities.

Nancy was only half listening, her mind was on other things. Like John Decker, and the suddenly renewed relationship. She wondered if he really meant what he said, if he truly was going to stick around this time. Despite the passing years, the pain of his leaving for college without her never quite went away. Not that it would have been easy to go with him. Her father had passed away the year before John left town, and then, with no one else around to help, her mother increasingly relied on her to help in the Diner. Still, she would have found a way. But he didn't want her around. He made that very clear. So she stayed in Wolf Haven, nursed a broken heart, and eventually married Lenny Snider, who was, according to her mother, a better fit for her, although he drank too much and was quick to landing a backhander if she so much as looked at him the wrong way. The day he finally walked out, Nancy celebrated with a bottle of the most expensive wine she could afford. Now here she was, five years later, coming full circle with the man she wished she had married all those years ago. The man she wished had been Taylor's father instead of Lenny. But still a nagging fear remained despite his assurances. Decker still harbored demons. He went through so much between the death of his mother and the descent of his father into obsessive madness that he could hardly avoid that, but it seemed there was more. He hadn't told her everything, but she knew enough to know that he didn't come back to Wolf Haven because he missed his hometown. He was running when he left, and he was still running when he came back.

So where did she fit in? Nancy wasn't sure yet, but she would need to find out soon, because she could feel herself falling for John Decker all over again, and that scared her, just a little.

Chapter 39

THE GARAGE WAS A MESS. Decker almost tripped twice, fighting his way past junk that he probably should get rid of. Most of it came from his parent's old house. Until a few years ago it was in storage, but since his garage was mostly empty, it seemed to make more sense to move it there so he could sort through it and decide what to keep and what to consign to the trash. Now all he needed to do was find the time, and the inclination.

He moved several pieces of old furniture and finally came across what he was looking for. A battered three-drawer filing cabinet containing old case files from years before. He opened the filing cabinet and flicked through the tightly packed manila folders until he located the one he was looking for. He pulled the file free and went back to his study, placing it next to a dusty brown document storage box sitting on his desk.

He opened the file and leafed through the yellowing sheets of paper within. The first sheet was a police report. He recognized the face that peered back at him from an old photograph paper clipped to it. It was his mother, looking just as she had the day she died. In the doorway behind her hovered a small unrecognizable figure, mostly in shadow. He knew who that child was, because he remembered standing there and watching his father take the photo. He examined the image, a sense of loss overwhelming him. His mother looked so happy, a broad smile upon her eternally youthful face. Less than a month later she would be dead.

There were other photos too, tucked in behind the paperwork. His father did not take these. They were the handiwork of a forensic photographer. He made a conscious effort not to look at those, for he knew what they would contain. It had taken several years of therapy to overcome the grisly sight of his mother's ripped up body and he harbored no desire to revisit that particular hell.

He moved on past the crime scene pictures, to a police report scrawled in scratchy untidy handwriting, probably that of a deputy, and read it. There was nothing new in the document, nothing he did not already know. Nothing that could help him now.

Next he turned his attention to the storage box. Until a few hours ago, he hadn't laid eyes on this box in years. It sat tucked away on a shelf in the attic. Inside were his father's notebooks and papers, most of them from the time after his mother died and before his father's death several years later. They were a sad record of a broken man's descent into paranoia and despair, and Decker could not bring himself to view them. Until now.

He lifted the lid from the box, ignoring the musty odor that rose from inside, and looked within.

Inside were several spiral bound notebooks. He recognized them as the same type he used to take to school, but English homework and Math problems would not fill these.

He pulled out the top one and opened it, peeling back the cover. His father's handwriting jumped off the page, faded but still readable. He scanned the text, read a few lines, but there was nothing of use. Just the ramblings of a fevered mind pushed beyond breaking. In some spots the writing was barely legible, but what he could decipher was nothing more than wild accusations and crackpot theories.

He flipped through a couple more pages, but it was more of the same. He wondered what he was doing. The box, and the notepads it contained, were bad news. All he was doing was dredging up a past he spent years struggling to make peace with. Decker still recalled what it was like after his mother's death, and he remembered these notebooks. His father would scrawl in them constantly, almost automatically, jotting down whatever random thoughts came upon him. At first the notepads were a way to cope with the loss and record his feelings. A suggestion of the town doctor. But they became so much more.

Decker sighed. This was useless. He should have known better than to think there was anything here. There was no connection between what happened then and what was occurring now.

He picked up the notebook intending to drop it back into the box, but as he went to close it his eyes picked out two words amid the jumble of nonsense, words that jumped off the page because they were even crazier than the rest of the scribbled rantings.

'Loup-Garou.'

Decker stared at the page, stunned.

He didn't believe for one second that a monster born of folklore and superstition killed his mother back then, but apparently the idea crossed his father's mind, more than once too. When Decker flipped through the remaining pages of the notepad he picked out the words a dozen more times.

It was ridiculous, of course. The Loup-Garou was a story, nothing more. A spin on the classic werewolf, a person could summon the beast through witchcraft, becoming the wolf for up to one hundred and one days, often to reap vengeance on those they perceived as having wronged them.

Decker closed the notepad and returned it to the box. This

was a futile waste of time. Whatever answers he hoped to find in those moldy, yellowed papers were not there, only old questions, and right now there were more pressing issues to resolve. He could wallow in the ghosts of the past some other time.

He picked up the box lid, intent on returning the box to where he'd found it. He was about to drop the lid back into place, when his eye caught something he hadn't noticed previously. Pushed down the side of the box, wedged between the inner wall of the container and the old notepads and papers, was a small rectangular envelope.

He plucked it out and looked at it for a second, turning it over in his hands. The envelope was decades old, much like everything else in the storage box. There was no writing on it, nothing to show what might be inside, but it was thick. His curiosity peaked, Decker examined the flap. The envelope wasn't sealed, but years of damp conditions had moistened the glue just enough to hold it closed. He pushed a nail under the flap and pried it back, careful not to damage the contents inside. He reached in, his fingers closing over brittle paper, and pulled out a wad of browned slips with faded text.

Newspaper clippings.

He laid them out on the table, handling them with a gentle care borne from years dealing with crime scenes and evidence, then sat back and cast his eyes over them.

The clippings were from about the time of his mother's death, something he confirmed from a dateline on one article, but to his surprise, they were not about his mother. Instead, they described other killings, all with a similar modus operandi, and all from towns within a fifty-mile radius of Wolf Haven. In the margin of one clipping, dated about two weeks after the attack on his mother, two words were written in his father's scratchy handwriting. He read the sentence, his heart racing.

'Same beast?'

So his father thought whatever mauled his mother had

attacked other people too. What's more, they never caught the creature responsible.

The similarity to the present was too much to ignore. Still, he didn't know how any of this helped him track down and catch the beast, and frankly, his father's conclusion that the killer was a werewolf didn't help the situation. He couldn't call in the State Police or FBI with a story like that, not unless he wanted a free vacation in a padded room.

A rumble of thunder shook the house. The light above the table flickered. The weather was growing worse. He could hear the rain pounding on the windows, the wind catching a distant gate, slamming it back and forth.

The storm was coming, and somewhere out in that howling rain, amid the pine trees and brush, a ruthless killer ran free. He had work to do, and not much time to do it, but not tonight. Tonight all he wanted was to feel the warmth of Nancy's body next to his, her lips as she kissed him, her touch as she held him.

He gathered the clippings together and returned them to the envelope, then placed it back in the box. There was nothing here of much use, at least not right now. Whatever truths the old documents hid would have to wait for another time. He picked up his car keys, threw on his jacket, and left the house.

Chapter 40

DECKER PULLED UP to Nancy's house, steering the cruiser past Cassidy's Diner and bringing the vehicle as close to her door as he could, before putting his hat on and making a dash for the shelter of the front porch.

He reached out to ring the doorbell, but there was no need. Nancy opened the door and pulled him in, her face a picture of relief. "Thank god you're back. I was so worried about you. What with this weather and all."

"I'm fine," Decker said.

"You're drenched," she exclaimed. "We need to get those clothes off you before you catch your death." She guided him toward her bedroom at the back of the house. "I was starting to think you wouldn't return."

"Sorry." He peeled off his jacket, which was wet not only from the dash to Nancy's porch but also from the time spent out at the Gas and Go, then removed his sodden shirt. "I came back as quickly as I could."

"I know." She pulled at his belt, releasing the buckle. "Take your pants off. I'll put them in the dryer."

"Is Taylor any better?" Decker fought his way out of his

pants. The fabric stuck to him and he almost fell over, but Nancy steadied him.

"Not really. I went up to see her after you left, and she was already awake. She was reading old text messages from Jake over and over. I gave her some more pills, and that seems to have knocked her out again for now. I increased the dose so she should be good until morning."

"Taylor will recover. Give her time." He slipped an arm around her waist and kissed her, their lips lingering together as if neither one of them wanted the touch to end. "Come on, let's go to bed."

"That sounds nice." Nancy nodded. "I should put your clothes in the dryer and check on Taylor, just to make sure she's okay."

"Alright, but don't be long." Decker watched Nancy cross the room, enjoying the way she looked in the black negligee that barely reached her knees. He wondered if she had put the garment on in anticipation of his return, or if it was something she wore regularly. Either way, she looked damned good.

On her way out, she grabbed a cotton robe and wrapped it around herself, and then she disappeared from view. He heard a creak or two as she ascended the stairs, and another as she made her way along the corridor to Taylor's room.

He made himself comfortable on the bed, and closed his eyes, thankful to be somewhere warm and dry. When he opened them again Nancy had returned. She stood at the end of the bed, a wry smile upon her face. She tugged at the belt that held the robe closed and slipped it off, then slid the straps of the negligee off her shoulders and let it fall to the floor before joining him.

Chapter 41

JEREMIAH BOUDREAUX HADN'T MOVED in almost two hours. He sat perched on the edge of the sofa, a box of old photographs open on the coffee table in front of him. The photos were mostly Polaroids taken decades before, others were from his old Pentax 35MM. Faded color images of Terry smiled up at him from yellowed photographic paper. One showed his son at age 10 riding a bicycle on the dirt road outside the trailer, another pictured Jeremiah, Terry and Pamela, a happy family, posing together on a beach somewhere. It was probably Pensacola, the only vacation they ever took together.

A bottle of liquor sat on the floor next to the couch. It was still full. At first all Jeremiah wanted was to drain the bottle, hoping it would burn away the pain, but when he lifted it to his lips, he knew the hooch would not have any effect, not tonight, and so he placed it down on the ground, and left it there, a silent witness to his torment.

A dull fire burned inside the old man as he sat on that couch, an anger that mixed with the grief to form a blinding, seething pain that he could not see beyond.

Hours before, in a fit of wild rage, he tore through the

trailer, knocking things over, kicking furniture, punching anything in his way, breaking crockery and ornaments. He screamed curses, some at Terry for getting himself killed, others at Floyd, who was surely as much to blame as the beast that had ripped the men apart. He even cursed himself for allowing Terry to get mixed up with the old moonshiner at all. It was only when he came upon the box of photographs that he finally cried, taking the photos out one by one, remembering each moment as if it were yesterday. Finally, even the tears dried up. He opened the liquor and sat in the silence of his trailer, and as he did so the rage seethed like a serpent coiling around his heart. He knew what he must do. He reached for the phone, dialed a number, spoke to the person on the other end for a moment, and then repeated the process a couple more times. Afterward, he went to the kitchen closet. This was where he kept his rifle. He withdrew it and stood awhile, letting the gun comfort him, before pulling open the trailer door and stepping into the howling, rain-soaked night.

Chapter 42

FOR THE SECOND time that day, they made love. Afterward they lay in each other's arms, neither one speaking for the longest time.

It was Nancy who broke the silence. "Promise me nothing will happen to you." She rolled over and looked at Decker, her hand resting on his bare chest.

"Nothing's going to happen to me. Why would you ever think it would?"

"Because you're going to go after whatever is killing people." She put her head on his shoulder. "It's your job."

"And I have a big gun." He stroked her hair, letting his fingers play through the soft strands. She smelled like fresh cut roses. "You worry too much."

"I don't think so. You don't even know what it is."

"Not yet." Decker wondered if Carol had sent the claw off for testing. "But we'll figure it out."

"Just be careful." Nancy pleaded. "I don't want to lose you, not now."

"I'm not going anywhere." Decker soothed her. "Except to pee." He swung his legs off the bed. The floor was cold on his bare feet. He headed for the bathroom. When he returned the bedroom was empty.

She was probably checking on Taylor. He went back to the bed and sat down.

And then he heard a crash.

He jumped up and grabbed his gun. His pants were still in the dryer, so he wrapped a towel around himself and ran from the room.

"Nancy?" He tore down the corridor into the living room, but she was not there. He turned right, into the kitchen, his gun raised, ready for whatever awaited him. Nancy was standing at the sink. The smashed remains of a drinking glass littered the floor next to her. Decker lowered the gun, snapped the safety, and placed it on the kitchen worktop. "What happened?"

"There was something out there."

Decker followed her gaze. "Outside the window?"

Nancy nodded. "I went upstairs to look in on Taylor, then came in here for a glass of water. When I looked out the window, it was just standing there, looking right back at me."

"What was?" Decker hitched the towel up to prevent it from slipping off and moved her aside. "What did you see?"

"I don't know. An animal of some sort. It was enormous."

Decker peered through the glass, but all he saw were the vague outlines of trees and the silhouettes of a few distant buildings amid the gloom. "There isn't anything there now."

"I know what I saw, John. It was right outside the window." Nancy was shaking. "It looked straight at me."

"Can you describe it?"

"It was hard to make out the features, but it had a long snout. I could see the tips of white teeth in its mouth, like it was curling its lips back. The eyes though, they were the worst. Two yellow slits."

Decker remembered the description Taylor had given of the animal in the woods. "Stay here." He went to the laundry room, opened the dryer, and took out his pants, pulling them on even though they were still damp. He grabbed his jacket, picked up the gun, and made for the front door. "Don't move."

"What are you doing?" Nancy asked, panicked. "You can't go out there."

"I'll be fine." Decker held up the gun. "If there's anything snooping around, I'll take care of it." Still, he couldn't help feeling a flicker of apprehension. Floyd and Terry had a gun. It didn't do them any good. He, however, was a trained law enforcement officer. He was also on the alert, while the moonshiners were probably half drunk and taken by surprise. He reached out and gripped the dead bolt, pausing for a moment as he collected his wits, then snapped it open and stepped out into the night.

The weather had gotten worse. No sooner had Decker stepped from the shelter of the porch, than he was instantly soaked yet again. Worse, gusts of wind blew stinging rain into his face, making it hard to see. He blinked to clear the water from his eyes and crept toward the side of the house. It was dark here. He wished he had a flashlight. There was one in his cruiser parked in front of the house, but that would have meant going back inside and getting the keys, and he did not want to waste the time. If he had any chance of catching this thing, he needed to hurry.

The side yard was an obstacle course. He bumped his shin on a BBQ grill, sending it toppling to the ground. A little further on he stepped around an enclosed trailer, the words Cassidy's Catering fading away on the side, a leftover from Nancy's ill-fated event business, which, it turned out, Wolf Haven did not have a great need for.

Beyond that he could see a pile of pavers, some plant pots, and several other things hard to make out in the gloom.

He found the back of the house. Light from the kitchen window spilled across a wide expanse of what once might have been a lawn, but was now nothing more than rain soaked dirt. He kept the gun high, ready for whatever might come lumbering out of the blackness, but his eyes could find no movement, no monsters waiting to provide an encore of the carnage at the Pump and Go. The yard was empty.

One thing he did notice was the height of the windows. Like many houses in southern Louisiana, the building sat on concrete block footings, with a crawlspace underneath to account for floodwaters. There was no way a regular sized animal could have been up there. Whatever Nancy saw peering in at her through the kitchen window must have been at least seven feet tall. He was not sure he wanted to confront a creature that large in the darkness, even with his gun. He backed up, deciding discretion was the better part of valor, and retreated to the front of the house, keeping his eyes open for the slightest movement as he did so.

When he got around front again he took the steps leading up to the porch two at a time and hurried inside, closing the door and bolting it, feeling safer as he did so.

Nancy watched from the hallway. She looked relieved.

"There's nothing out there," said Decker, walking past her to the bedroom where he stripped off his clothes and grabbed a towel, rubbing his hair dry and wiping the wetness from his face. "Whatever you saw is long gone."

"I hope so." Nancy shuddered. "Don't do that again."

"What?"

"Leave me alone like that."

"I won't." Decker drew her to him and kissed her gently on the forehead. "I promise."

Chapter 43

JEREMIAH BOUDREAUX WAITED at Floyd's camp in his pickup with the engine running, rain pelting down on the windshield with a sound like hundreds of fingers drumming all at once, and Led Zeppelin's Your Time is Gonna Come playing on the radio. He wasn't listening to the music. He just couldn't be bothered to turn it off.

He sat there for what felt like an eternity, consumed by thoughts of Terry. Anger and frustration boiled inside him, accompanying his grief like a fine Cabernet would go along with a rare steak, not that he'd ever even contemplated such a pairing.

When he saw the twin beams of another set of headlights coming up the track leading to the clearing, he shut off the engine and climbed from the cab, taking the rifle from the passenger seat as he did so.

The newcomer pulled up in a dark colored Camaro. Jeremiah could not make out the exact shade, but he had seen the car often enough to know that it was Mystic Teal Metallic, although the years in the sun had taken their toll, reducing the paintwork to something more akin to dark gray. Behind the

Camaro, a Jeep Wrangler bobbed up the trail and came to a halt.

Three men climbed from the cars, each brandishing a weapon. Bobby Boudreaux, his cousin, carried a shotgun. He also sported a pistol, stuck deep into his belt, the grip visible above the waistline, the rest nothing more than a slightly phallic bulge disappearing into his pants. That seemed to Jeremiah like a good way to blow your junk off, but what the hell, he probably didn't use it much anyway ever since his wife Shirley ran off.

Gill Maynard, the driver of the Jeep, cradled a lethal looking short-barreled rifle, which he carried as though it was the most precious thing in the world, one hand on the stock, the other curling around the stubby black muzzle. His passenger, Duke Timmons sported a double barrel sawed-off shotgun that dangled from one hand, pointing down toward the dirt, the casual manner of the gun's transportation belying the sudden death that awaited anyone unfortunate enough to find themselves at the business end of the weapon.

If this were any other night, there would be some raucous banter exchanged already, and possibly a few good insults, the stuff guys said to each other when they met up for a night of carousing. But not tonight. This particular evening, Jeremiah met the occupants of the vehicles with less than his usual enthusiasm. Then, he wasn't here to play poker and down a few bottles of gut rot. Tonight was all about Terry.

"Sorry to hear about your boy." Gill was the first to speak.

"A real tragedy." Duke Timmons added.

Bobby said nothing, merely placing a hand on Jeremiah's shoulder, the gesture saying more than words ever could.

"Yeah. Thanks." Jeremiah nodded, looking between the three of them. "Terry would appreciate you guys coming out here to do this for him. He really would."

"He was family." Bobby spoke up. "Family do for each other."

Duke looked toward the impounded still. "Besides, the damn thing killed Floyd, and he made the strongest hooch for a hundred miles."

"You're not wrong there." Gill said, and Jeremiah had to agree with him. Despite being a despicable specimen of humanity, a man who had all the charm of a skunk, he possessed a God-given talent for making liquor that would blow your socks off.

"Tasted like shit though." Duke added.

Again they all agreed.

"You sure we'll find this thing up here?" Gill asked.

"Sure enough," Jeremiah replied. "It was here yesterday. Damn thing walked right past me while I was taking a piss. Thank god I was in the latrine or it probably would have chewed me up too. I figure it must have a den somewhere hereabout."

"That's good enough for me." Gill said.

"We ready to do this?" Duke raised his gun and pointed it toward the woods.

"Let's go catch us a wild animal," Bobby said, spitting a gob of saliva out of the side of his mouth. He watched it hit the ground and mix with the rainwater and mud. "Time to get some revenge for our Terry." He slapped Jeremiah on the back. "Ain't that so."

Jeremiah nodded again and looked toward the woods. "So what are we waiting for?" He hitched the gun up and stepped toward the woods.

The four men moved forward slowly, their guns at the ready. Under the cover of the trees it was darker than any of them had imagined, especially since the moon was behind a thick layer of storm clouds. At least the trees deflected the pounding rain, not that any of them were dry by this point.

"We should split up," Gill suggested. "There's a lot of ground to cover and we'll stand a better chance of finding this thing."

"Are you crazy?" Bobby hissed. "That would be suicide."

"He's right. We should stick together, at least for now," Duke said.

"Keep it down. We'll never find anything if you keep yapping." Jeremiah shot them an angry look.

Bobby opened his mouth to reply, but when he saw the look on Jeremiah's face he decided against it. The old man had a legendary mean streak, and he didn't intend on running foul of it, especially right now. He had a feeling Jeremiah would not think twice about using the rifle for more than hunting wild animals, given his current state of mind.

They walked on in silence, all four of them listening for any sound that didn't belong, but only the sounds of frogs and the sporadic hoot of an owl greeted their ears.

At first they skirted the camp, following the perimeter as it curved around, but then, directly behind the old cabin, they moved away from the clearing, pushing deeper into the forest. The ground was wet and treacherous underfoot, and more than once one of them slipped, reaching out for a tree trunk to steady themselves.

The forest was thick with brush and low branches, making it hard to navigate, but soon they came upon a trail, and followed it deeper into the woods, away from the camp. For an hour the three men searched, conversing only when necessary, until they reached a point where the trail split in two, the twin paths forking off at forty-five degrees from each other. Unsure which way to go, they caught their breath.

"Which way now?" Duke adjusted his raincoat, pulling it tight to keep the water out.

"We'll take the left fork first. If there's nothing doing there, we'll circle back and explore the other path," Jeremiah said.

Gill spoke up. "This is crazy. We're never going to find anything out here. There's just too much ground to cover. Damn thing could be anywhere."

"I'm not ready to give up just yet." Jeremiah kept his voice low. "My boy's dead because of this thing, and I want to see it suffer."

"We don't even know what we're looking for." Gill protested.

"Doesn't matter." Jeremiah's shook his head. "I'll know it when I see it."

"Another hour, then I'm done," Bobby whispered. "I want to get out of these wet clothes and get some vodka down my gullet. We're wasting our time out here."

"We're done when I say we are," Jeremiah hissed, annoyed at the change in mood. A few hours ago, everyone was eager to find the beast that killed Terry. Now they were just about ready to give up. "And I ain't said it yet. Let's keep going."

"Not before I take a piss," Duke said. "Anyone else need to shake a leg?"

"Dammit Duke, why couldn't you do that before we got in the woods," Bobby said.

"I did. I need to go again."

"Goddam. Well, make it quick," Bobby grumbled. "I don't want to be standing around out here like this. It feels wrong."

"Just give me a minute will you," Duke stepped away and disappeared into the thick undergrowth, pushing his way through until he disappeared between the pines.

Chapter 44

DUKE TIMMONS LEANED his shotgun against a tree and unzipped his pants, freeing himself and aiming at the ground, even though he could not see exactly where he was urinating, and let forth. The relief was instant.

He wondered how long they would have to stay out here, tromping around the woods in the pouring rain. He was cold and wet, and wanted nothing more than to get back home and climb into bed. It wasn't like they stood much chance of finding the animal that attacked Terry, anyway. There must be thousands of acres of pinewoods stretching across this part of the state in all directions, and it could be anywhere. Chances were that it was miles away by now, and even if it wasn't, it was like looking for a needle in a haystack.

Hell, for all he knew Terry deserved what he got. They probably pissed the damn thing off somehow. The boy was dumb as dishwater, and Floyd Benson was not too far behind. Rumor was that the years of drinking illegal hooch had addled what little brains god gave him and having tasted the stuff on more than one occasion Duke thought it was probably the truth.

That was beside the point, though. It didn't matter if

Terry brought it down upon himself, or if the beast was still around. What mattered was that Jeremiah wanted to go chasing ghosts in the middle of the night, and Duke knew better than to say no, so here he was, stuck in this miserable forest until his friend either found what he was looking for, or gave up.

Duke finished up and shook to remove any errant drops of pee, then slipped it back in his pants. He was about to zip up when something moved in the darkness between the trees. It was nothing much, just a slight shift in the gloom between the pine trunks, almost imperceptible, but it was there, none-the-less.

He froze, looking to pick out the cause of the movement, his ears straining to pick up any unusual sound, but there was no sign of whatever he thought he had seen.

Feeling vulnerable, Duke backed up.

It was probably just his imagination. There was nothing to fear. Yet strangely, he was afraid. The hairs on the back of his neck stood up, and he felt his heart pounding in his chest.

He reached for the gun, eager to rejoin the rest of the group. At that moment there came a faint shuffling off to his left. He swiveled, scanning the woods for the cause of the sound, and then he saw it, crouched between the trees, watching him with curious fascination, yellow eyes, little more than slits, holding his gaze.

The beast tilted its head to one side, never breaking eye contact with him.

Duke held his breath, unable to look away, although every fiber of his body urged him to flee. He closed a hand around the gun, picking it up as slowly as he could to avoid spooking the creature.

The beast reared up, as if sensing what was about to happen, and took a step forward.

Duke raised the twelve-gauge, aimed, and pulled the trigger.

The recoil sent him staggering backward. He reached out and steadied himself against a tree trunk. When he looked up, the beast was still there, only now it wasn't just watching him, it was closing the distance between them at an alarming rate.

He lifted the sawed off gun and fired a second round, peppering the beast with shot. He might as well have been throwing popcorn at it for all the good it did.

Duke backed up and broke open the gun. He fumbled to reload, pulling fresh cartridges from his pocket, but before he could slide them into the breach, the creature lunged.

Chapter 45

WHAT THE HELL?" Bobby turned toward the gunshot.

"Duke." Gill took a step forward.

A second shot disturbed the silence, followed by a sharp, brief scream, then nothing.

Jeremiah lifted his weapon and charged toward the gunfire. He plowed through the undergrowth, all thought of stealth abandoned. Gill and Bobby hitched their weapons and followed suit, pushing at the thick undergrowth and stepping over tangled vines that threatened to trip them at every footfall.

It didn't take long to find Duke. He lay sprawled on the ground, his gun several feet away. His head lay twisted to the side, his eyes wide open and glazed over. A haze of blood covered his lips and chin. His neck was now a gaping hole, torn skin flapping over exposed gristle and bone. One arm was bent backwards at a crazy angle. The other covered his face in a defensive posture.

"Holy Jesus," Bobby muttered. "What have you gotten us into, Jeremiah?"

"He's dead." Gill glanced around, nervous.

"No shit, Sherlock." Jeremiah rubbed his forehead with the back of his hand.

"We have to get out of here." Bobby turned to face their rear and raised his gun. "This place ain't safe."

"No one's going anywhere." Jeremiah wheeled around, his face flush with rage. "Damn thing's close. We need to finish it."

"Are you crazy?" Gill protested. "Look what it did to Duke, man. He fired off two shots. We all heard them. It still ripped him to shreds."

"Yeah, well, there are three of us." Jeremiah walked to the shotgun, picked it up, and kneeled next to the corpse. He found the cartridges still clutched in Duke's hand and pried them free with a grunt. "We have it outnumbered."

"What the..." Gill shook his head. "This is bullshit."

"I agree," Bobby chimed in. "Duke's a fine shot, and it still got him. We should get the hell out of here while we still can."

"No one's leaving." Jeremiah raised himself up. "You want to turn tail and run, you gotta go through me first." He leveled his rifle toward the two men.

"Okay, okay. Let's all just calm down." Bobby shifted his weight from one foot to the other, nervous. "There's no need to be pointing guns at us, Jeremiah. We're all in this together."

"Seems to me that the pair of you would rather scamper like scared little bitches than avenge my Terry." Jeremiah shook his head. "Never pegged ya'll for cowards."

"Damn right we're scared," Bobby said. "You should be too. Duke's dead for chrissakes."

"And standing here like a bunch of sissies ain't gonna bring him back," Jeremiah said. "Now come on, let's go put an end to this." He took a step forward, finally bringing the muzzle of the rifle down. He pushed between them and walked off without a backward glance.

"Should we follow him?" Gill kept his eyes averted from the bloodied corpse.

"Hell no. I've had enough of this," Bobby said. "I'd rather get shot in the back by Jeremiah than end up dinner for whatever did that." He hitched a thumb toward Duke.

"I don't know." Gill said. "It don't seem right to leave him out here, all alone."

"Stay if you want. I'm off." He turned, taking a step back toward the trail, and then stopped, his eyes alighting on a dark shape in the bushes several feet away, a shape that almost blended in with the surrounding forest. Almost.

"What the hell?" He took another step, trying to make out what he was looking at. He tugged on Gill's arm. "Do you see that?"

"See what?" Gill turned toward his friend.

At that moment the creature stepped from the shadows. They had found what they were looking for, or rather it had found them.

Chapter 46

SEVEN FEET of sinew and muscle covered by cracked, leathery skin rippled as the beast moved toward them, low on its haunches. It studied them through pale yellow eyes, the pupils twin vertical slits, black as coal. It sniffed the air with a long canine muzzle that sported rows of needle-like teeth capped by two large downward protruding fangs.

Bobby raised his gun, almost dropping the rain-slicked weapon in his haste. He wrestled it under control and brought it up, aiming squarely at the beast.

Gill aimed his weapon, hands shaking so much he wondered if he could even hit the beast.

At that moment, the creature pounced. It barreled forward in a blur of speed and landed between the two men, claws finding Gill's chest and opening him up from neck to waist before he had time to react. Bobby ducked instinctively, but the creature's sweeping arm caught him alongside the head, sending him sprawling. The shotgun flew from his grip and landed somewhere in the thick vegetation that lined the forest floor.

Jeremiah turned at the sudden commotion, his eyes flying wide. He stood transfixed, the rifle in one hand, Duke's shotgun in the other, but made no attempt to fire either weapon.

Gill let out a strangled screech and dropped his gun. He raised his hands to stem the flow of blood. He tried to speak, but all that came out was a rasping, gurgled hiss.

The creature circled, eyeing the stricken man, then snatched him up and raised him from the ground. Gill hung like a rag doll, limp and useless, his mouth opening and closing in silent agony. Blood bubbled between his lips. His eyes bugged from their sockets. He pawed uselessly upon his assailant, but he was too far-gone to strike a meaningful blow. Then, with a swift sideways motion, the beast sank its muzzle into the soft flesh of Gill's stomach, and ripped a chunk free, sending a spray of blood and guts across the forest floor.

"Jesus Christ, man, help us." Bobby crawled toward Jeremiah. "It's killing Gill. Shoot the bastard. Shoot it now."

Jeremiah loosened his grip on the shotgun, his eyes never leaving the horror unfolding before them. The weapon slipped from his fingers and slid to the ground, falling away with a dull thud. He made no attempt to lift the rifle clutched in his other hand.

The beast discarded Gill's bloodied, lifeless carcass, and padded toward Bobby, jaws wide.

"Oh, please no." Bobby kicked at the earth and pushed himself backward. Panic flared in his eyes. "Dear God, help me."

The beast kept coming.

Bobby reached down and pulled the pistol from his pants. He raised it and fired, the bullet smashing into a tree wide of its mark. He fired off another round, but his hands were shaking too much. It whizzed wide left, hitting somewhere behind the beast with a thud. He hoisted the gun a third time. The creature sprang forward as Bobby pulled the trigger; the bullet finding the spot the creature occupied a second earlier.

Then the creature was upon him, jaws snapping closed around his chest.

Jeremiah stood and watched as the beast finished its grisly task. When it turned toward him, yellow eyes blazing, he dropped the rifle. A sob escaped his throat. Then Jeremiah's bladder released. Warm liquid flowed down his leg and pooled on the ground at his feet. A final ignominy in the face of the beast that had killed his son.

The creature padded forward, drawing within a few feet of Jeremiah. Then it stopped, observing him with cool intelligence.

They faced each other, monster and man. And then, as if deciding he was not worth the bother, the creature turned and walked off.

Jeremiah sank to his knees. He did not try to pick up his gun or follow the beast. Instead, he put his hands up to his face and cried.

He remained there for an hour or more, surrounded by the bodies of his dead friends. Finally, oblivious to the torrent of icy rain, he staggered to his feet, leaving the discarded guns where they lay, and walked back to Floyd's camp.

Chapter 47

ON MONDAY MORNING, after leaving Nancy with a promise that he would check in on her later, Decker drove to the sheriff's office. When he entered, Carol greeted him with her usual smile, but he could tell by the look on her face she was anything but cheerful.

"Morning, John. The coffee is fresh. The pastries, not so much."

Decker poured a coffee and eyed the box of donuts open on the counter. They looked as stale as Carol claimed them to be. "Is it too much to ask for a good donut shop in these parts?" he said, picking one up, then putting it back with a scowl on his face.

"Probably," Carol said. "Do you want the bad news first?"

"What's the alternative?"

"The worse news."

Decker sighed. "Alright, spill it."

"The Coroner confirmed that all four victims, Jake Barlow, Floyd Benson, Terry Boudreaux, and Benny Townsend, were killed by the same animal. Bite radius, tooth marks, and wound patterns are identical. And here's the kicker, there's no match to their database of known animals. It's not a bear, a bobcat, or an alligator. They even looked at exotic animals like lions and tigers and still didn't get anywhere. In short, the coroner's stumped. It was a wild animal, and that's about as much as anyone can tell us."

"Figures." Decker already suspected as much. "I assume that was the bad news, so what's the worse news?"

"That storm in the Gulf. It's getting bigger. Last night it was a tropical storm, now it is a category two."

"That explains the shitty weather."

"There's more. The weather service has narrowed the projected landfall."

"Let me guess," Decker said. "It's coming right for us."

"You got it," Carol replied. "There's a seventy percent chance it will come ashore between Terrebonne Bay and West Cote Blanche, then head inland. We're slap bang in the center of the cone. If it keeps to that path, the hurricane will be here in fourteen hours, give or take."

"Fantastic. This town goes a hundred years with nothing going on, then everything shows up on my watch," Decker said. "Looks like we have some work to do."

Chapter 48

JEREMIAH BOUDREAUX SAT on the floor of his trailer, back pressed against the front door. He hadn't moved since the early hours of the morning.

The previous night had been a disaster. Three of his friends were dead, their lifeless, shredded corpses still out in the woods. Worse, he'd watched them die, too afraid to lift a finger in their defense. He should have fired on the beast, killed it. It was right there, a few feet from him. He could have done what he went into the forest for in the first place and avenged his son, but instead he just dropped the guns and stood with piss running down his legs.

He was a coward, and he hated himself.

Jeremiah replayed the scene over and over in his mind, looking for some clue that might help explain why he was still alive. The beast should have ripped him apart, shredded him like pulled pork, but it walked off instead. He wasn't even a worthy enough adversary for the beast to bother killing him.

Jeremiah moved finally, lifting himself up and shuffling to the bedroom. His legs felt weak and stiff. They tingled as the life came back to them after hours on the cold floor, but he didn't care. He peeled his damp clothes off and dumped them in a pile, then flopped down on the bed and closed his eyes. He could not remember when last he slept, but it was a long while ago, he knew that much.

The bed was comfortable. Much better than the floor.

He pulled the sheets up and settled in, wanting more than anything to drift off and escape the reality of his situation for a few hours. Yet sleep proved elusive. His mind would not shut down. Images of Terry, and the shattered bodies of Gill, Duke, and Bobby, hounded him. He saw the beast again and again, those yellow eyes and hungry, slathering jaws. It haunted him. He pushed the thoughts from his mind, forced himself to relax, and eventually, little by little, succumbed to a deep slumber. But even this offered no respite. The beast crept into his dreams and terrorized him some more, while outside the weather grew worse ahead of the approaching storm.

Chapter 49

DECKER SPENT the morning and a good part of the afternoon making sure the folk of Wolf Haven were aware of the approaching storm. Already many of the businesses on Main Street had boarded up lending the town an air of abandonment that Decker found unsettling. The usually busy main thoroughfare was quiet with only the occasional pedestrian braving the worsening weather. The small supermarket at the edge of town was one of the only businesses still open. The parking lot was full, and Decker suspected that there would be little left on the shelves come morning. Having done all he could, Decker returned to the sheriff's office and hurried inside.

Chad was at his desk toward the rear of the room, leaning back in his chair with his feet up. His eyes were closed, hat pulled low over his forehead. He appeared to be napping.

Carol was at the computer. She looked up as he entered. "Storm's getting worse. Looks like it will be a category three before long."

"Don't you ever have any good news?" Decker asked as he took a seat behind his desk.

"Actually, I do. Sort of. We got the results back from the tests on that claw."

"That was fast."

"They rushed it through after I reminded them that lives were on the line." Carol stood and walked to the coffee station. She picked up the carafe and turned back to Decker. "Want one?"

"Sure. I have a feeling it's going to be a long night."

Carol poured two coffees and handed one to Decker then took the other to her own desk. She sat down and sipped her drink.

"Well?" Decker glanced at her impatiently.

"When the test came back it showed human DNA."

"Huh?" Decker shook his head. "That claw was clearly not human."

"I know." Carol leaned back. "The lab knows it too, which is why they ran a second test figuring the first one must have been contaminated. Same result."

"How is that possible?" Decker asked.

"It's not," Carol said. "According to the test results our claw is from a person, which of course is impossible. The lab is going to try again tomorrow after they've sanitized every-thing and checked their equipment. In the meantime, we are no closer to knowing what type beastie is running around our woods than we were before."

"I guess we wait, then. At least with the storm raging outside our mysterious killer won't have much chance to strike again."

"Speaking of the storm, a lot of the houses around town are old, especially the ones out near the swamps. They were not built to withstand this kind of weather."

"I was thinking the same thing myself," Decker said. It would be prudent to activate our emergency response plan and get a shelter open."

"I'll bring up the plat maps. There's a bunch of places out

by Bayou St. Edwards. Those folks will need to get to higher ground, for sure." Carol turned back to the computer and started typing. She glanced toward Chad. "I could use some help."

Decker picked up a sheet of paper and balled it up. He drew his arm back and tossed it at the deputy. The paper cannonball hit the dozing man on the nose.

Chad sat up with a start. "Hey, who threw that?"

"Rise and shine, sleepyhead. There's work to do."

"I wasn't sleeping," Chad grumbled. He dropped his feet off the desk and sat up straight. "What's going on?"

"If you'd been paying attention, you would know." Decker nodded toward Carol. Why don't you lend a hand identifying who we need to evacuate ahead of the storm."

"What are you going to do?"

"I'm going to make some calls. There's a lot to do and there isn't much time."

Chapter 50

MAYOR BEAU THORNTON drove the two blocks from his house to the sheriff's office. It was early evening, but already the sky was so dark it might as well be the middle of the night. Dirty, roiling storm clouds scudded overhead, bringing with them bands of rain that lashed the windshield so hard the wipers could barely keep up.

He was not a cheerful man. Between the spree of killings and the swiftly approaching storm, his safe re-election bid was fast slipping from a sure thing to a shot in the dark. Less than thirty minutes before, the governor, sensing the need to cover his own ass, declared a state of emergency, which meant there was little chance the storm would miss them. It also meant that Mayor Thornton needed to look like he knew what he was doing. Thornton would have to act fast, look like he was on top of it, if he wanted to keep the title of mayor much longer. When he arrived, he found the entire town police force rallied there. Of course, that only comprised the sheriff, his Deputy and the dispatcher, Carol.

Chad looked up when he entered. "Hi there, Beau."

"Please address me as Mayor."

"Sure thing Beau, whatever you say," Chad replied.

Decker suppressed a smile.

"What can we do for you, Mayor?"

"You tracking this here storm that's coming in?"

"Sure are," Decker replied. "Looks like it's going to be a wild ride. Maximum sustained winds of one hundred twenty miles per hour."

"So I hear," Thornton said.

Decker spoke again. "The storm is moving fast and growing in size. We have two hours, maybe three, before the weather is too bad to do anything."

"What are we looking at?" The Mayor raised his eyebrows. "How bad?"

"Downed power lines and flooding are a given. Plus, there are buildings hereabouts already in rough shape. There's no telling what those winds will do to them."

"Or trees," Carol said.

"That too." Decker frowned. "We're looking at a lot of downed trees."

"Christ." Thornton threw his hands up. "When it rains, it pours, pardon the pun."

"It is certainly going to pour." Decker leaned on the counter. "Which is why I want to open a shelter. Evacuate the more vulnerable folk in town to a safer structure."

"Absolutely not. People will not want to abandon their property. We'll put a curfew in place, keep everyone indoors."

"Fine," Decker said. "But this thing is big, there could be casualties, even deaths."

"That won't help your re-election bid," Carol chimed in.

"Damned election."

"I know," Carol said. "Having to deal with pesky distractions like the democratic process."

"Alright already. You win." Thornton threw his hands in the air. He looked like a kid who just lost their lollipop. "Voluntary. Not mandatory."

"That's what I thought you'd say," Decker said. "I've

already placed a call to the school board. We can use the high school gymnasium. That will easily hold several hundred people. We'll issue an alert on the emergency broadcast frequency."

"A lot of folk won't hear that," Thornton said.

"The local radio station will run PSA's too," Carol said. "It's required if they want to keep their license."

"Still won't reach everyone."

"I know. That's where the Sheriff's Office comes in. We'll round people up the old-fashioned way if we have to." Decker motioned toward Carol. "You should go to the school and get things set up there. Take the Mayor with you."

"Now hang on a darn second," Thornton complained. "You can't order me around."

"You're right. You can come with Chad and myself, if you prefer. Your choice," Decker said. "I just thought you would want to be at the gym to show how much you care for folk. Being Mayor and all."

"Well, since you put it like that, maybe the school is a better place for me."

"That's what I thought." Decker smiled. "Let's get started then, and hope we don't run into whatever is killing folk while we're at it."

Chapter 51

THE BAR WAS EMPTY, but Ed Johnson stayed open anyway, partly because there was nothing better to do, and also because he hoped that at some point a customer would show and keep him company.

It was unlikely though, given the double blow of the foul weather and a killer on the loose, but he lived in hope. If nobody showed up by 9 p.m. he'd call it a night and shut the place down, but not just yet.

On the TV above the bar, the local weather station showed a graphic of the storm churning toward the coast. Already larger than originally forecast at a category three, it had the potential to grow even more thanks to the warm Gulf waters. A timeline graphic predicted the storm making landfall in the next three hours, which meant things were going to get worse before they got better.

Sick of the doom and gloom, he snatched up the remote and flicked through the channels until he came to a comedy show, grabbed a bottle of whiskey, and poured himself a drink.

He settled at one of the bar stools, put the bottle on the bar, and downed the drink, enjoying the burn as it made its way to his stomach. He poured another and repeated the process.

Despite the alcohol, it was hard to relax. He expected the door to fly from its hinges at any moment and the Loup-Garou to come charging in, jaws wide, ready to devour him. He could not banish the beast from his mind. Ever since seeing the creature two nights ago, he felt unsafe, uneasy. It was a shame the sheriff didn't take the beast seriously. Of all the people in town who should have an idea what was going on, it was Sheriff Decker. After all, his own mother was a victim. But like everyone else, John Decker was closed minded, unable to accept a truth that did not fit his limited beliefs.

There was nothing Ed could do about it except have another drink and hope the alcohol would blot out those memories.

He lifted the bottle and poured a third shot. He was about to gulp it down when the TV blared a burst of high-pitched sound. He looked up, startled. An emergency announcement scrolled across the bottom of the screen. Seconds later, the audio alert started. Ed listened for a moment, then returned his attention to the bottle of whiskey. There would be plenty of time to evacuate later. Right now, he wanted another drink.

Chapter 52

CHAD STEERED his cruiser through the quickening storm, hands tight on the steering wheel to counter the buffeting wind. Visibility was less than ten feet. Once in a while the night sky lit up as a finger of lightning raced across it, followed by the ominous rumble of thunder. To the left and right lay dense swampland. It hugged the road, as if trying to reclaim the asphalt. Up ahead was a fork, the left side tracing a route that would eventually lead a person all the way to New Orleans, while the right pushed deeper into the woodlands atop a hammock, a mostly dry protrusion of land that fought to maintain dominance over the murky waters that surrounded it.

Chad veered to the right. A mile up, the blacktop ended, and the road devolved into a muddy dirt track. He fought the steering wheel as the car shifted and slid on the slick surface, wheels spinning on the over-saturated ground.

Up ahead, the lights of a cabin glowed brightly through the darkness. Chad drew closer and parked up a little way from the building.

From this distance, he could make out more detail. It was

nothing more than a shack, with fading paint and a sagging porch. The boards were rotten, some hanging lopsided from rusted nails. A thick mat of pine needles and dead branches carpeted the roof.

He reached behind his seat and found his hat before climbing from the car. He hitched up his belt and took a deep breath. Annie Doucet was the last person he wanted to see, but the sheriff wanted everyone rounded up. The old woman did not have a TV or even a radio. That meant driving out here to warn her of the worsening storm in person. Personally, he didn't care if she went to the storm shelter or not, but it wasn't up to him.

He made his way toward the dwelling, apprehensive, his palm resting on the butt of his gun, which made him feel a little safer. When he reached the building, he paused for a moment to compose himself, then stepped up to the porch.

"Annie?" He rapped on the door. "Annie Doucet? This is Deputy Chad Hardwick."

There was no answer.

He knocked again. "Annie, are you in there? It's important I talk to you. Could you come to the door, please?"

She must be inside. The old woman rarely left her filthy hut, making the trip to town only when absolutely necessary. Besides, he could see her clapped out old Dodge sitting under a nearby oak tree.

"Annie?" He called her name once more, deciding that if she did not respond this time he would just head back to town. He had no desire to be out in this weather and if she did not want to be civil, that was up to her.

He was about to give up and return to the warm comfort of his cruiser when the door creaked open a few inches. A pair of dark eyes observed him through the crack.

"What do you want?" Annie's voice was brittle, full of phlegm.

"There's a storm heading this way, Miss Doucet, a big one. Sheriff thinks you should come on down to the school. We've set up a shelter in the gymnasium." He suppressed the urge to flee back to his car. She gave him the creeps with those watery eyes that seemed to look right through him.

"A shelter. Isn't that nice and civil of Sheriff Decker."

"Miss Doucet-Annie-you really shouldn't stay here. The storm is packing some pretty high winds and you'll pardon me for saying so, but this here cabin isn't exactly built to code."

"It'll survive the storm, I'm sure," she said. "We've been through worse."

"Be that as it may, you should go to the school." Chad doubted the old structure would survive the storm, and if it didn't, well, that would just be one less thing for the bulldozers to tear down when the new road went in.

"I'll come to the school when I'm good and ready," she said, keeping the door where it was, never bothering to open it wide and invite the sodden deputy in out of the rain.

"Well, that's good to know." Chad didn't want to be there anymore. The more distance he could put between himself and Annie Doucet, the better. Something about her made his skin crawl. No wonder they said she was a witch. "I'll leave you in peace then."

He backed up and stepped down from the porch, not wishing to turn his back on the old woman, keeping her in sight until he was almost at the patrol car.

As he climbed in she shouted to him over the gusting wind, her voice surprisingly strong given how feeble she sounded just a few moments before. "You tell Mayor Thornton that I'll see him there."

He closed the car door without bothering to reply, then reversed up and turned around, pointing the cruiser back toward town. When he glanced in his rearview mirror Annie was on her porch, watching him.

He pushed the accelerator to the floor, eager to put as much distance between himself and the crazy old woman as possible. He was halfway to town before the writhing unease in his gut faded.

Chapter 53

WOLF HAVEN WAS A GHOST TOWN. Decker was pleased to note that most people had either made their way to the shelter at the school, or battened down the hatches to ride out the foul weather.

The storm was growing worse by the minute; the winds starting to batter hanging signs and awnings. Trees bowed in the gale, their trunks resisting the onslaught for now. Smaller branches and pieces of dead wood were already falling to the ground. He wondered how long it would be before a tree came down or a falling branch took out the overhead power lines.

Ahead of him, in the road, a loose trashcan careened from one sidewalk to the other. Somewhere further away an unsecured door banged back and forth, the noise mixing with the patter of the rain and occasional thunder claps.

He slowed and cruised along Main Street. Most of the businesses had either put up hurricane shutters or nailed plywood across their windows. Only the County Line Saloon still had a light burning. Ed's car sat out front. Decker pulled in behind it and opened his door, fighting the wind as he stepped from the vehicle. He held his hat and rushed to the door. Locked. He banged with a fist, hoping the sound would carry over the howling wind. There was no answer. Either Ed couldn't hear, or he'd left already for the gym, leaving his car behind. Decker turned and ran back to the cruiser, then headed toward Cassidy's. He drove up the side lane toward the house at the rear. This too was dark and empty. Good. Nancy must have retreated to the shelter with Taylor. He would catch up with them there.

He pulled back onto Main, checking the road one more time, and then took a turn around the back streets. The houses showed no sign of occupants, most of them boarded up to save the windows from flying debris. He continued on, his blue and red lights bouncing from the sides of buildings, illuminating everything in an ethereal strobing glow.

At one point, when he was halfway through an intersection, something bolted in front of the cruiser. He stopped and watched a fat tabby bound across the road and slink under a home, pressing its body through a broken trellis to gain access to the crawlspace beyond. No doubt it was seeking somewhere dry and safe to ride out the impending onslaught, just like everyone else in Wolf Haven. For a moment he considered stopping to retrieve the animal, but it was probably halfway under the house by now, and he doubted it would come to him even if he found it.

Decker reversed and pulled a U-turn. He'd done all he could. The weather was deteriorating at an alarming rate. Like the cat, he should find shelter. He gunned the engine and steered the car in the school's direction.

Chapter 54

ANNIE DOUCET WATCHED the police cruiser recede down the road and become one with the storm. She hesitated a moment to make sure the deputy kept going, then stepped back inside the shack. She moved toward the table, upon which sat a copper bowl containing a brownish sludge.

She lifted it to her lips and drank deeply.

No sooner had she done so than she felt the change approach. The bowl fell and clattered to the floor. It rolled away and came to rest beneath the table.

She staggered to the cabin door and flung it wide, the pain already flaring in her extremities. No matter how many times she did this, it still hurt more than anything else she'd ever experienced.

Annie collapsed to her knees, rain soaking her hair, her clothes. It didn't matter. She fumbled with the buttons of her blouse and ripped it off, then removed her skirt.

Naked, water streaming across her sagging flesh, her silver hair flying wildly in the wind, she waited.

She didn't have to wait long. The burning pain in her arms and legs spread across the rest of her body. Annie doubled over. She threw her head back and screamed, a long, drawn-out wail of agony. Unable to do anything else, she curled up into a ball and gritted her teeth against what she knew would happen next. She could feel herself slipping away, the beast taking over. Her muscles rippled, grew. Limbs stretched and twisted. Bones cracked and reformed themselves to a new configuration.

Then it was over.

The creature that had been Annie only moments before raised itself up and let out a bellow of animalistic rage. No longer feeble, the beast leaped from the porch and landed several feet away. It sniffed the air, stretched its limbs, and took off running toward town as the rain fell and lightning cracked the sky.

Chapter 55

JEREMIAH BOUDREAUX AWOKE to the sound of someone calling his name. He opened his eyes, blinking away the last remnants of sleep, before turning to look toward the voice.

There, in the shadows a few feet away, stood his son Terry, looking just like he had the last time Jeremiah saw him.

"I thought you were gonna sleep forever," Terry said. "Christ, but you snore like a five hundred pound hog looking for truffles."

"How are you here?" Jeremiah lifted himself up on the bed.

"Now what kind of dumb question is that?" Terry ran a hand through his hair, then dipped into his pocket and pulled out a packet of cigarettes. He plucked one from the carton and put it to his lips. "I live here, don't I?"

"You're supposed to be dead," Jeremiah said. "That deputy told me he found you all chewed up in the woods."

"When did you ever listen to what the law had to say?" He struck a match and lit the cigarette.

"I just thought–"

Terry cut him off. "Good job out in the woods, by the way. Getting everyone killed. Real nice."

"There was nothing I could do," Jeremiah protested. "It all happened so fast."

"Bullshit. You had the damn thing right there in front of you, and you didn't even try to kill it. You pissed yourself like a sissy instead."

"Now hang on—"

"You're lucky it didn't kill you, too. Guess it didn't think you were much of a threat." Terry took a drag off the cigarette and exhaled, a cloud of white smoke hanging in the air between them. "You can still kill it though, show it who's boss, if you've got the balls that is."

"I'll do it, Next time it'll be different."

"We'll see." Terry took another drag of the cigarette. "You'll need to wake up first though."

"What?"

"You're still dreaming, stupid." Terry flicked the cigarette toward him. "Wakey, wakey."

JEREMIAH'S EYES FLEW OPEN. A peal of thunder rumbled overhead, shaking the trailer. He looked around, hoping to see Terry there, but the room was empty. He felt a pang of disappointment. The dream had felt so real, it was like he was actually talking to his dead son, even down to the air of disrespect the boy carried around with him, and he could swear there was a faint odor of cigarette smoke lingering in the room. He wasn't dreaming anymore, of that he was sure. The other thing he was sure of was that when he crossed paths with the beast again, it would be a whole different story.

He swung his legs off the bed and stood up, pulling on a pair of jeans and a denim shirt, then kneeled and pulled a long box from under the bed. He opened the box and lifted out the rifle inside. This was a special gun, a gun his father had given him when he was just a boy. He'd learned how to shoot with this gun, and now it would get justice for his son.

Outside, beyond the trailer's thin walls, the wind howled, and the rain poured down, but Jeremiah didn't care. The creature was out there somewhere, just waiting for him, and he thought he knew where.

Chapter 56

THE STORM WAS COMING in hard and fast by the time Ed Johnson concluded that he should head to shelter at the school. The wind was already rattling the bar's windows, and a few minutes ago something had skittered across the roof. It was probably a branch, but it made him nervous. There was a large oak tree near the rear of the building. If that came down, he would be flattened. Better to vacate than end up squashed.

Besides, the bottle was empty, and he didn't think it was a good idea to crack open another. At least not here. He was buzzed. The whiskey had left him with a pleasant glow that took the edge off his unease. He should take a bottle with him to keep it that way. Come to think of it, he might as well take a case. The huddled town folk at the gymnasium would probably welcome a stiff drink or two. And also, Ed reasoned, there was no point in leaving it here. If the roof came off the building his stock would be ruined, and if it didn't, a case of liquor was a small price to pay to earn the town's good will.

Ed discarded the empty into the recycling cart and turned the lights over the bar off, then made his way to the stockroom and unlocked the door. This was where he kept the majority of his liquor and wine. He stepped inside and paused. Metal shelf racks lined the walls. Upon these were rows of bottles. One side contained cases of red and white wines. The other held the hard alcohol, rum, vodka, and gin. And of course, whiskey. Ed considered himself something of a connoisseur and liked to keep a good selection even though most of his customers preferred beer. He lingered at a row of small batch bourbon made in the hills of Kentucky. This felt too good to give away. Instead he pulled down a case of Jim Beam and turned back toward the door.

He'd barely taken a step when he heard a crash from the bar.

Ed faltered mid-step. The storm must be getting worse. Had something come through a window? He bent and placed the case of whiskey on the ground and stepped past it. He was about to reenter the bar when something made him stop. He was overcome by a sudden sense of foreboding. He stopped and listened, ear straining to pick up any aberrant sound over the howling wind and pounding rain. He stayed that way for a minute or two, giving into his own unease. Then, when he didn't hear anything, the prickling disquiet faded. There was nothing here. He was just spooking himself.

Ed turned back to the whiskey and hoisted it in his arms then made his way back into the tavern. He placed the whiskey on the bar surveyed his surroundings. That was when he noticed the front door standing open. Rain slanted in, slicking the floor. The doorframe was busted around the dead-bolt, the wood splintered and broken. Something had smashed its way inside. But that wasn't what made Ed's heart jump into his throat. It was the muddy paw prints that trekked from outside and did a circle of the room.

The intruder was not human.

Ed swallowed hard. The prints were too big to be a dog.

But they were definitely canine. He could see where the pads had rested. And the size of that gait... There was only one thing Ed knew that could leave tracks so large.

The Loup-Garou.

He glanced around nervously, expecting to see the beast hunkered down watching him, but he was alone. Even so he didn't want to stay here one minute longer. He scooped up his keys and hurried around the bar, then snatched up the case of whiskey and made his way to the door and stepped outside.

The rain was coming down in sheets, slicing almost horizontally through the frenzied wind, but Ed didn't care. He rushed to the car and deposited the liquor onto the back seat. Then he dashed back to the tavern and pulled the door closed. It wouldn't lock, but at least it stayed shut. He secured it as best he could with fumbling hands, all the while feeling vulnerable. He was an easy target out here alone on the street. That done, Ed ran to the car. He jumped in and slammed the door, then depressed the locks. Even then he didn't feel safe. He took his phone out. Decker hadn't believed him about the Loup-Garou, but it was out there. He had to warn the sheriff. The beast could be anywhere by now. Who knew what it was up to? But when he tried to place a call, there was no service. Ed stared at the phone in disbelief. He was truly on his own. Now more than ever, he wanted to get to the school. He dropped the useless phone on the passenger seat and pushed the key into the ignition. The car made a rattling cough but did not start. He tried again and this time the engine sprang to life. With a silent prayer of thanks, he pushed the gear stick into reverse and backed out of the parking bay, then swung the wheel hard to the left. He was about to slip the gear stick into first when he saw a flash of movement in his rearview mirror. He swiveled around and peered through the back window and for a moment he could have sworn there were eyes watching him out of the darkness. Eyes that burned yellow. But then, as quickly as they'd come, the eyes were gone.

Ed turned frontward again and put the car into gear. Then he pressed down on the accelerator and took off in the direction of the gymnasium, happy to get out of there.

Chapter 57

MAYOR BEAU THORNTON stood at the door and greeted the citizens of Wolf Haven as they entered the gymnasium. The spree of killings, and the storm, could not have come at a worse time given his re-election bid in the fall, but maybe it wasn't all bad. At least he was out meeting people. When God gave you lemons, he mused, you made lemonade.

Secretly he wished he were somewhere else. Anywhere else. Even so, he was in full politician mode. He smiled, made small talk, and let everyone know he was responsible for the haven they were currently enjoying - even if he wasn't.

God, I'd kill for a cigarette, Beau thought. He could not remember the last time he'd lit up, having quit the year before. As a vocal supporter of the local initiative to curb teen smoking, he could hardly partake of the habit himself.

"Evening, Beau." Charlene Riggs, owner of the town's only hair salon, ambled up, dusting rain from her jacket. Her bleach blond hair was matted to her scalp. The front of her blouse, soaked because she hadn't bothered to zip her coat, was plastered to her chest in an unflattering way that left little to the imagination.

"Evening, Charlene." Thornton motioned toward the

gym, eager to move her along. Mascara was running down her cheeks giving her the appearance of a bedraggled clown. For a woman in the beauty trade, he mused, she was not a great advertisement for her own wares.

"Got room for one more body in there?" Charlene glanced toward the crowded gymnasium.

"Well now, there's always room for you." Thornton flashed his best smile.

"That's mighty nice of you to say, Beau."

"Not at all. I was hoping you'd come along." He spoke the words before realizing he was not presiding over one of his frequent fundraisers.

"And here I am." Charlene tittered and brushed past him, into the gym.

Thornton watched her go, feeling a mite stupid now. He wondered how long the storm would last. Hopefully, it would pass over quickly, because he wasn't sure how long he could keep up the smiles and handshakes. Spending a few hours schmoozing at a wine and cheese social, or working a room to raise funds for his campaign was one thing, but spending an entire night locked in with these people? It didn't bear thinking about. There was only so much charm to go around, and he could feel his nerves fraying already. He pushed his hands into his pockets. He would get through it. There was no choice. Now if only he could stop thinking about that damn cigarette.

Chapter 58

DECKER SPOTTED Beau Thornton the moment he entered the school building. The Mayor was shaking hands and acting like the storm was a campaign social. What a jackass, he thought to himself.

"Evening, Sheriff," the mayor said as he approached.

Decker nodded a greeting. "I see you've been holding down the fort here, Beau," he said, wondering if Thornton could detect the note of sarcasm in his voice.

"Someone has to make sure the good folk of Wolf Haven are safe," he said, much louder than necessary. When he noticed a few people turn their heads his way, he spoke again. "You can always count on the Mayor's Office to handle things."

"Sure." Decker shook his head. "You keep up the excellent work, Beau." The man was nothing more than a part-time town clerk, and not a good one either. The rest of the time Beau Thornton acted as the town's only lawyer, drawing up wills, filing divorce papers, and dealing with whatever minor legal woes came his way.

"Always do, Sheriff."

"Yeah." Decker made his way into the gymnasium. It was bustling. He estimated half the town must be there. That was good, the more people that took shelter at the school, the less would end up in harm's way.

He paused and looked around, searching the throng. A pang of anxiety gripped him when he didn't pick out Nancy's face. She should be here by now, but he couldn't see her. There was no sign of Taylor either.

"Weather's getting nasty out there."

Decker turned to see Chad strutting toward him. He nodded in agreement. "Sure is."

"I swear, I almost got blown clear off the road." Chad said. He chewed a stick of gum with a lazy chomping motion. "Damned lucky I didn't end up in a ditch. There's no way that storm is only a cat two."

"Weather service is calling it a three now." Decker was pleased to see the deputy didn't have those stupid sunglasses hanging out of his shirt pocket, at least. "Did you have any problems rounding folk up outside of town?"

"Nah." Chad scratched his head. "Except for crazy old Annie Doucet. I tell you, there's something not right with that woman."

"Don't tell me you think she's a witch, too."

"Do I look like I'm eight years old?" Chad shook his head. "She sure is a weird one, though. Practically threw me off her porch. I just hope she didn't decide to stay up there in that hut of hers. Whole dang thing will probably collapse when the wind hits."

"She was warned. Nothing else we can do."

"I know," Chad said. "Next time around, you can drive up to the creepy cabin in the woods."

"Deal." Decker scanned the crowd, his eyes flitting from face to face.

"She's over by the refreshment table." Chad pointed toward the far end of the room.

"Who is?"

"Nancy Cassidy," Chad replied with a grin. "I swear, Decker, you are so obvious sometimes."

Chapter 59

ED GRIPPED the steering wheel tight and drove as fast as he dared toward the school. The rain was coming down so hard that he could barely see through the windshield even with his wipers on at full pelt. He turned off Main Street, taking a shortcut, and made his way through a residential neighborhood lined with shotgun houses on both sides. He was still shaken. The beast had been in his bar. Was it looking for him? If he hadn't been out back grabbing that case of booze, he might be dead right now. That was a sobering thought. Still, the school would be safe. There was no way the creature would find him there, especially in a storm such as this. It had probably already slunk back to where it came from.

He turned onto another street and eased off the gas a little. The houses were boarded up and mostly dark. Only a few had dim light flickering from within. Most people, he guessed, had taken refuge at the school. The town was eerily deserted. The nagging unease crept back, and Ed cast a quick glance into his rearview mirror once again. He turned his attention back to the road too late to avoid a metal trashcan that had taken flight. He slammed his brakes on and swung the wheel hard to the right. Ed realized his mistake even as the car started to slip sideways. He fought to regain control but between the wind and the slick road surface it was a losing battle. The car continued to slide, careening sideways across the road, until the front wheels bumped over the curb and the front end dropped hard into a drainage ditch. Ed was thrown forward, his head smacking into the steering wheel. The seat belt dug into his chest, then threw him back into the seat. He groaned and brought his hand up to his forehead. He could feel unconsciousness overcoming him. He pulled at the door but it would not open. The world was growing dark. He was losing the battle to stay awake. Ed sank back into the driver's seat and starred through the car's side window. The last thing he saw before passing out was a dark shape slinking down the road toward the school. The Loup-Garou was on the way, and there was nothing Ed could do to warn anyone.

Chapter 60

BEAU GLANCED AROUND. The steady stream of people arriving at the school had slowed to a trickle, nothing more than a few stragglers. There was no point standing at the door anymore. He briefly contemplated entering the gymnasium, but then he would need to smile and make nice with the town folk all over again, and he wasn't sure he could stomach that right now. But the school was a big place, and there were plenty of quiet corners to sneak a quick smoke. He tapped his trouser pocket to make sure his cigarettes were there, the ones he'd kept all these months since giving up, just in case. Then he slipped away while the corridor was empty and hurried to the double doors leading into the main school building.

With the gymnasium out of earshot, the school was silent and deserted. He breathed a sigh of relief, happy to be away from the crowd of sheltering townsfolk. Still, it felt weird to be so alone in a place that usually hummed with life, especially with the storm raging outside and rain drumming on the roof.

"Get it together, Beau." He spoke aloud. The sound of his own voice broke the spell and pushed the unease away.

He wandered along the corridor, footsteps echoing. To the left and right he passed empty classrooms. When he was far enough away from the gym he stopped, leaned against the wall, and pulled out a cigarette.

The last time he lit up in this school it ended with a week of detention, and a good thrashing from his father, who held firm to the old saying, spare the rod and spoil the child. The sting of the strap wasn't the worst of it though. The look of disappointment in his mother's eyes hurt far more than any physical abuse. But that was a long time ago. His father, the mean old bastard who liked to beat his son with a belt, was rotting in his well-deserved grave, and his mother spent her days in a nursing home outside Baton Rouge, where she stared at the walls and, on the rare occasions he visited her, called him Jimmy. He found this particularly infuriating since the only person of that name she ever knew was their next-door neighbor forty years before. She could remember him, but not her own son.

He fumbled in his pocket for a book of matches, opened it and tore one out. He was about to light the cigarette when the sound of breaking glass reached his ears.

He paused, the unlit cigarette between his fingers, wondering if he had imagined it. The sound came again. This time there was no mistake.

He cursed. A tree must have come down and bust through a window. That would cost a pretty penny to repair, he was sure. Not to mention the water damage. They would have to rip up the floor, install new drywall, and rewire. The flood damage would run into the tens of thousands, and who knew if the school's insurance policy would cover it all. That would leave his office responsible for finding the money to put everything right, and the town coffers were already low. Truth be told, if the highway spur didn't bring in more business – and the business taxes that came along with it – they would be broke within two years. It wouldn't be the first time a town filed for bankruptcy.

He contemplated going back to the gymnasium and

finding John Decker, but then thought better of it. The sheriff didn't like him, Thornton could tell. He didn't want to look like a sissy in front of the man. Maybe he should go look for himself and assess the damage, before calling in the cavalry. The corridor had two windows, one at each end, and they were fine, so that left the classrooms. He cracked the closest door open and peeked in, flicking on the light. Everything was in order, the tables and chairs neatly arranged in rows. The windows, which stretched the length of the far wall, were all intact. Rain lashed the panes, turning the world beyond into a murky surrealist painting. He closed the door and tried the room across the hall.

Again, nothing.

He proceeded down the corridor, moving from room to room, but found nothing.

He reached the last door. A plastic sign fixed to the wall next to the doorframe read 'Teacher's Lounge.'

He eased the door open.

The room sported three windows, each equally spaced. Rain blew through the furthest of the three, soaking the carpet and furniture. Papers flew everywhere, caught in the howling gale. Glass shards littered the floor. There was no sign of whatever broke the window. No fallen tree limb or other debris that might have punched through it. He reached for the light switch, but then thought better of it. Water and electricity did not mix well. He pulled his hand back and surveyed the situation with the light that spilled in from the corridor. There was a lot of rain coming in. He would have to go back and find someone to board up the window before the storm inflicted any more damage. The school must have a maintenance guy, and if he were lucky, that person would be in the gymnasium right now. He just needed to find them. Even the janitor would do.

Problem solved.

He was about to close the door and hurry back toward the

gym, when he noticed something that should not be there. It hunkered in the corner. A lighter black within the shadows. Then it moved. A dark shape that stretched and elongated.

Beau froze. Deep within him, a primal sense of self-preservation stirred. It told him to run and not look back. Except he couldn't. His legs refused to work. A creeping sensation wormed up his spine. Whatever hid in the corner was not natural. It should not exist. How he knew this, Beau had no clue. Maybe it was some primordial instinct, the same one that taught children to be afraid of the dark, or maybe it was just a premonition. Whichever it was, he did not want to be there anymore.

Then the shape moved. Slinking from the darkness.

The shadows fell away like a thinning mist.

Beau tried to look away, but could not. A fascinated horror compelled him to watch.

Then he noticed the pair of unblinking yellow eyes, watching him back with malevolent intent, and Beau Thornton finally found his feet.

Chapter 61

DECKER FOUND Nancy at the refreshment table brewing a new batch of her world famous coffee. He smiled. No matter how bad things got, Nancy would always make sure the town didn't run short of hot beverages.

"Well hello there, stranger." He slipped his arms around her.

"Hi yourself." She twisted around and kissed him, her lips lingering on his. Afterward, she looked up into his eyes. "I've missed you."

"Me too." He brushed a stray hair from her forehead. "I would have gotten here earlier, but…"

"You were out keeping the town safe."

"Something like that. How's Taylor?"

"Oh, pretty much the same. She's not talking, keeping all her feelings bottled up. I was hoping she would have come out of herself by now."

"She will," Decker said. "Time is a great healer."

"So people keep telling me." Nancy rested her head on his shoulder. "She took off the moment we got here. Said she wanted space. She's been moping in the corner over there ever since."

Decker followed Nancy's gaze. Taylor was propped with her back against the wall ignoring the surrounding activity. "It's only been a few days since Jake died. Give it time."

"I know," Nancy said. "At least she's stopped obsessively reading his text messages."

"There you go." He held her close, relishing her warmth as she snuggled into him.

"I suppose." She looked up at Decker, a tear welling in her eye.

He wiped the tear away and kissed her forehead, unsure what else he could say. Instead, he opted to change the subject. "So, how about a cup of your delicious coffee?"

Chapter 62

TAYLOR CASSIDY WATCHED the sheriff and her mother hugging. It didn't seem fair. They had each other when she didn't have Jake. In fact, almost everyone in the gymnasium had someone, and she was alone. Maybe she was really still on the banks of the swimming hole, lying there in her bikini, sleeping in the sun with Jake next to her. Any moment Jake would wake her up and drag her into the cool, clear water. He would pull her close and kiss her, and tell her he loved her.

Only he wouldn't, ever again. Because she was not sleeping up at Sullivan's Pond, she was in a hot, cramped gymnasium with half the town, while outside a hurricane raged.

She suppressed a sob.

More than anything, she wanted to be alone. The sympathetic stares and platitudes only reinforced the reality of her loss. One by one, half the town had approached her with variations of the same trite words. That everything would be better soon and just give it time. Screw that. Nothing would ever be the same again.

Her mother and the sheriff were over at the refreshment table, preoccupied with each other. They were paying scant attention to Taylor. She had been told to stay close, but Taylor could not stand another moment in that room. The cramped space, full of people, was suffocating. She rose to her feet and weaved through the throng, making her way toward the door. The Mayor was no longer there. The corridor was empty. She stepped out of the gym and turned left toward the main building. It was quiet here, and the further she moved from the gymnasium, the better she felt. She wandered a while, enjoying the peaceful solitude. Until she ended up in front of the lockers. Whether she found her way here purposely, or by accident she was not sure, but either way, she knew exactly who owned the locker she now faced. She reached out, her fingers playing with the padlock. She hesitated a moment, unsure if she should open the locker. She knew the combination. It was the month and day of Jake's birthday.

0216.

She dialed the numbers and pulled the lock free, then opened the metal door.

The locker contained precisely six items. Three textbooks, an empty lunch box, a denim jacket, and a photo stuck to the inside door. The photo showed her and Jake several weeks prior, outside of a movie theater in New Orleans. She remembered the night well. It was their second date. After the movie, Jake held his phone out and took a selfie of the two of them from arm's length. He said he wanted to remember that night forever.

She took the photo down and turned it over. On the back, in Jake's scrawling handwriting, were three words.

Best night ever.

She slipped the photo into the back pocket of her jeans, wiping away a tear.

The books were nothing special. One was a math book, Calculus AP. The other two were history texts. She ignored them and pulled out the jacket. She was with him the last time he wore that jacket. It was a baking hot day, humidity off the charts, so he stuffed it in the locker rather than carry it around. She raised the garment to her nose, burying her face in the soft fabric.

It still smelled like Jake.

She stayed that way for a moment, savoring the lingering sense of Jake, then slipped the coat on and pulled it tight around herself. Wearing this jacket made her feel closer to him, as if he were there next to her, holding her. The sense of loneliness eased a little. She closed the locker door and reset the padlock, intending to return to the gymnasium. She should have let her mother know where she was going. She didn't want to worry her. But before she could take a step forward, there was a muffled bang somewhere outside, and the lights went out.

Chapter 63

MAYOR THORNTON RAN. He fled as fast as his legs would carry him.

The beast crouched in the teacher's lounge was on the move. Tables skidded sideways and chairs tipped over as it pushed past them. Something crashed to the floor and shattered. A coffee cup maybe, or a plant pot.

The beast was giving chase.

Thornton slowed and turned, risking a backwards glance. When he saw what emerged from the teacher's lounge, he wished he hadn't. A bolt of fear shot through him.

The thing was monstrous.

Standing erect on thick hind legs, the beast rippled bulging muscle under tough leathery skin. Wicked claws pawed the air below a head straight from his worst nightmares. The creature opened its mouth and let out a guttural bellow, displaying rows of razor-sharp teeth.

He ripped his eyes from the terrible visage and ran once more, tearing down the corridor in a blind panic back in the gymnasium's direction. If only he could make it there, he would be safe. The sheriff had a gun. So did his half-baked deputy, Chad. They would surely kill the creature. Thornton felt a flicker of hope. Maybe he would be alright. He'd barely formed this thought when the power went out.

The sudden darkness was absolute.

Thornton skidded to a halt. His heart pounded against his ribcage. His breathing sounded way too loud. From somewhere to his rear, the creature emitted a low growl. Padded footsteps drew closer. Even though he couldn't see, Thornton knew he could not stay there. The beast was stalking him, and he sensed it could see much better in the dark than he could. Thornton took off again, slower now, lest he trip and fall. That would be the end, for sure. He felt his way along the corridor, using the wall as a guide, until his hands came to rest on a doorframe. It must be one of the classrooms. He closed his palm over the door handle and slipped inside, quietly as he could.

The classroom was no better than the corridor. When the power went out, so had the outside street lamps. Where before light had spilled through the windows, now they were indistinguishable black squares against a deeper gloom. He bumped into a table; the legs scraping the floor with a high-pitched squeal. He waved his arms around, feeling his way past obstacles until he came to the teacher's desk. With a flush of relief, he kneeled on all fours and crawled underneath, into the space where the chair usually went.

He held his breath.

There was no sound. No sign of movement.

Was the beast still following him? He could not tell. Maybe it didn't see him duck into the classroom. It was probably still prowling the corridor outside, searching for him. He would hide here and wait it out. Someone would miss him eventually, and then the sheriff would come looking. Thornton pushed back as far under the desk as he could and waited. The steady patter of rain on the roof, and wind-blown tree branches tapping against the windows, were his only company. At length, he wondered if the beast had passed by. He hadn't heard it for several minutes. Maybe it was heading away from him and toward the gym. Then a nasty thought occurred to Thornton. If it reached the gymnasium, there would be a bloodbath. He had no clue what the beast was, or where it had come from, but it wasn't friendly. He was sure of that. The gathered citizens of Wolf Haven were defenseless. If he didn't warn them, a lot of people would die. There was only one problem. The creature was surely between himself and the gym. He would never get around it, and if there was another way back, Beau didn't know of it. Not to mention the darkness. He couldn't even see. It would be foolhardy to even attempt a return to the gymnasium.

Better to stay where he was.

Then he remembered the cell phone in his trouser pocket.He could call Decker and tell him what was heading their way. Thornton almost cried with relief. He reached down and took his phone out. Then another nasty thought struck him. Had the cell towers gone down when the electric cut out? He would find out soon enough. Please work, he prayed, taping the screen to wake the device. Let there be a couple of bars.

The phone lit up, illuminating the cramped space.

The beast was right there, yellow eyes glaring at him.

It hunkered motionless on all fours, snout inches from his face. Thornton met its gaze, and in that moment he could have sworn a flicker of satisfaction passed across those unfathomable sulfurous eyes.

He jolted backward, smacking his head on the back of the desk. A squeal of fear escaped his lips.

The creature let out a snort. Its breath reeked with the carrion stench of death.

Its jaws opened, lips curling over black, putrid gums to display rows of monstrous teeth. Saliva dripped to the floor.

Thornton gagged and recoiled.

He let go of the phone.

It fell to the floor. The room plunged back into blackness.

Then the screaming started.

Chapter 64

WHERE'S TAYLOR?" Nancy cast her eyes around the gymnasium.

Decker shook his head. "Last time I saw her she was sitting against the wall near the water fountains."

"She's not there now." A note of panic rose in Nancy's voice.

"I'm sure she's around," Decker said. "Maybe she went to the bathroom."

"Maybe."

"Why don't you call her?" Decker said. "She's sure to have her phone. You know, being a teenager and all."

"Good idea." Nancy pulled a phone from her pocket and lifted the phone to her ear. She frowned. "It's not ringing. Call failed."

"Try again."

She dialed again and then shook her head. "No wonder it's not connecting. I don't have any service."

Decker checked his own phone. "Me either. The storm must have knocked the cell towers out."

"Great," Nancy said. "She should be back by now if she went to the restrooms."

"Don't panic. I'll look around. She can't have gone far."

"That would be great." A look of relief flashed across Nancy's face.

"Stay here. I'll be back." Decker said, then made toward the retractable gym bleachers. He climbed the steps, avoiding the huddled groups of people that occupied the benches. A few glanced up, annoyed, as he passed, but no one said anything. He continued on to the top and stopped. Here, Decker had a good vantage point to survey a wide swath of the gymnasium. He didn't see her. Frustrated, he descended to floor level and circled behind the seating. There were a few teenagers hanging out here. They moved off when he approached, the sight of his uniform enough to convince them to go elsewhere. He came out the other side and walked the room's perimeter, stepping between the groups of people clustered cross-legged on the floor, or huddled talking in hushed tones. He came up empty. Taylor was not in the gymnasium.

"I looked everywhere. She's not here," Decker said, returning to Nancy.

"We have to find her," Nancy said, a worried look upon her face. "She shouldn't be by herself right now."

"She can't have gone far." Decker placed a hand on her shoulder. "She must be in the school. Is there anywhere she would go, somewhere that means something to her?"

Nancy shook her head, then looked up at him, wide eyed. "There is one place."

"Where?"

"Jake's locker." Nancy led Decker out of the gym. "Come on."

"Do you know where his locker is?" asked Decker, following along.

"I have a good idea." Nancy approached a set of double doors that led further into the school. She stepped through, took off along the corridor. "Jake's locker should be this way."

"What are you going to say when we find her?" Decker

asked. "Maybe it's better to give her some space. She can't get into too much trouble."

"We need to find her," Nancy said. "Ever since the attack, I can't help feeling that I'm lucky she's still alive. If things had played out differently, she would be dead. It's not over yet. That beast is still out there. I can't lose her."

"You won't lose her," Decker said. "I promise."

"You don't know that." Nancy's voice faltered. "That monster that killed Jake came to our house. It looked in the window. I saw it. Why would it do that, unless it was looking for her?"

"It's an animal. I don't know why it came to your house, but it was a coincidence, nothing more."

"I hope you're right," Nancy said. They were at an intersection now, with a corridor running in each direction. She pointed left. "The lockers are this way."

Before Decker could respond, a loud bang echoed through the building. A second later the lights went out.

Chapter 65

TAYLOR STOOD IN THE DARKNESS, wondering what just happened. She waited, hoping the lights would come back, but they didn't. The only thing that still worked was an exit sign at the end of the corridor, operating on emergency power. Apart from that one beacon, darkness swirled thick and disorienting, while outside, the storm raged. She reached out and fumbled for the lockers to feel her way along. She knew the school well enough, and should be able to find her way back to the gymnasium even in the dark. She shuffled forward, taking slow, deliberate steps.

She had almost reached the glowing exit sign, when a warbling, terrified scream rent the air.

Then, as quickly as it began, the scream cut off.

Taylor froze, shocked by the suddenly terminated wail.

The darkness pressed in around her. Her heart pounded a mite too loud. The blood rushed in her ears. Something was here, she knew. It wasn't just the cut off scream, bad as that was. She could sense it. The air had become heavy, as if an invisible blanket had dropped. She was in danger. Taylor took off and ran headlong, all thought of feeling her route now abandoned. Her breath came as short staccato pants. Her footsteps echoed down the empty hallways. Leaving the gym had been a foolish idea. If it wasn't for her own wallowing self-pity, she would be safe right now. Decker would have protected her from whatever was out there in the blackness. Decker and his gun. He could just shoot at it. That wouldn't happen though. Taylor was on her own, at least for now. She prayed the lights would come back on. They didn't. Which left her little choice but to press on, blinded, through the gloomy corridors.

Until her foot snagged something unexpected.

She pitched forward, landing heavily. Her head cracked against the hard tile floor, sending a stab of agony down her spine. She moaned and rolled over, staring up into the inky blackness, afraid to move, knowing she must. She climbed to her feet and checked herself for injuries, wincing when she found the spot where her head had connected with the floor. She had broken nothing, a small mercy, but she would be sore for a few days.

She would have to be more careful despite the gnawing sense of danger that set off alarm bells in her head.

With a calming breath, Taylor reached out and found the wall once more. She had lost her bearings when she fell. Which way was she heading? Taylor didn't know. Aware she could not stay in one place, she picked a direction and continued on, feeling her way along. With luck, she wasn't moving toward whatever had elicited that bloodcurdling shriek. She had never liked darkness. There was always a nightlight in her bedroom at home. Now, alone in the darkened corridor, with no idea which way would take her back toward the gymnasium and safety, she could feel her panic rising.

Then, as if tasking pity on her, the emergency lighting kicked in.

The corridor lit up in a dim, bluish light. Enough illumination, at least, to see her way. Even better, she recognized her surroundings. A small sob of joy escaped Taylor's lips. Relief momentarily overpowered her fear. She would be back in no time. She took a step forward, eager to reach the safety of the gymnasium. She'd barely gone two steps before her eyes picked out a shape crouching in the shadows up ahead. A creature she recognized from Sullivan's pond. The beast that had killed Jake. And somehow, impossibly, it was here at the school, blocking her path. She drew in a sharp breath, swallowing the scream that was trying to force its way up. Because maybe it hadn't seen her yet. But then it padded from the gloom, yellow eyes fixed upon her, and Taylor knew it had.

She froze, caught in a moment of terrified uncertainty. The only escape route was in the wrong direction, away from the gym. She would be on her own. But there was no other choice.

Taylor backed up. Her skin prickled. The hairs on her neck stood up.

The beast emitted a low growl and lopped casually toward her, then broke into a trot.

Taylor let out a scream, then turned and ran. She fled headlong down the corridor, paying no heed to where she was going. Lockers flanked one side of the hallway. She slowed, just enough to take hold of an open locker door and pull, sending the unit crashing to the floor. Text books and papers spilled out.

Behind her, heavy footsteps indicated the beast was giving still chase. She risked a glance over her shoulder. The fallen lockers had done nothing to slow the beast. It was closing the gap. At the speed it was moving, there was no way she could outrun it for long. If she stayed in the corridor, the creature would catch her for sure. Her only chance was to lose it and hide until either the monster gave up or someone came looking for her. The question was, how could she evade it long enough to find a place to hide? And then the answer dawned on her, and it was so simple it just might work.

Adjoining doors leading from one room to the next linked all the classrooms on this floor. She could use that to her advantage.

When she reached the next classroom door she ducked sideways, then ran between the rows of desks, toward the adjoining door. As she did so, a nasty thought occurred to her, something she had not accounted for. The connecting door might be locked. She could already hear the beast approaching. If the door didn't open, she would be dead.

Taylor reached the door and grasped the handle, praying that it would turn.

She barreled into the room, slamming the door closed as she went, then weaved through that room into the next, where she dove under a desk.

In the previous room, the beast was searching. She could hear furniture scattering. A heavy thud as something fell. Breaking glass. Then a moment of silence.

Taylor waited, hardly daring to draw breath. Maybe her plan had worked, and she'd lost the beast. But then, as if to prove her wrong, the door burst open and the creature entered, snorting and huffing. She peered through a gap between the chair leg and the desk. She glimpsed the creature prowling between the rows of desks. It moved with slow, deliberate steps, hunting her. Taylor stifled a sob and held her breath. The beast sniffed the air, nose twitching as it picked up her scent. Then it turned toward her hiding place and looked right at her.

Taylor let out a desperate wail. She jumped up. The desk tipped over, scattering pens across the floor.

The beast observed her with cool indifference.

Taylor felt a surge of anger over the fear. This was the creature that took Jake from her. "Go to hell!" She screamed the words, tears streaming down her face. She picked up a chair and threw it with all her might. It glanced off the creature's back but did no damage.

The beast reared and let out a displeased growl. It advanced toward her, mouth agape.

Taylor backed away, slowly at first, but then she turned and fled, upending chairs and tables as she went. When she reached the connecting door, she turned and fled back into the previous room, bolting through it and into the corridor. Now she was back where she started.

Out of breath, legs aching from the exertion, Taylor pushed herself forward.

The beast skidded into the corridor and gave chase.

Up ahead was a restroom. Since she couldn't hide from her pursuer, she would need to slow it down to have any hope of living through the night. She put on a spurt of speed and barreled through the door. It banged back on its hinges. The restroom contained a row of three stalls separated by cubical walls. There was just enough space under each for what she was planning to do. She breathed a silent prayer that it would work, because if it didn't, there would be no escape. The beast would rip her apart as surely as it had killed Jake. She raced to the furthest stall, entered, and pulled the bolt across. She stripped Jake's jacket off with a silent apology and wiped her face with it, getting as much of her sweat on the cloth as possible. If the beast was tracking her scent, she would give it something to find. She discarded the jacket next to the toilet and pulled the flush to attract the beast's attention. That done, she dropped to her knees and squirmed under the partition to the next stall. When she reached the last of the three stalls, the one closest to the restroom door, she locked herself in and waited without flushing, barely daring to breathe.

At that moment, the beast reached the restroom. It crashed inside, ripping the door from its hinges and sending it flying, and moved toward the sound of the flushing toilet.

Taylor waited for the creature to pass by. She held her breath, expecting it to turn and find her at any moment, but it kept on toward the furthest cubicle. Trembling, she crept from her hiding place and crawled under the last partition wall.

The beast was at the far stall. It lowered its head and nudged the door. When it didn't open, the creature rammed it hard, sending the door flying back on its hinges with a bang. It stuck its head inside.

That was all Taylor needed. She sprinted toward the exit.

The beast sensed her escape. It roared with frustration and swung its head sideways, demolishing the next cubical. As she entered the corridor she heard more splintering. The last stall giving way as the creature extricated itself from the narrow space.

Taylor wasted no time putting as much distance between herself and the beast as she could.

She reached the end of the corridor and hesitated. If she went left, it would take her back toward the gymnasium, but if she went right, she would reach the woodworking shops. There were tools there, hammers, chisels, and all manner of sharp objects. She could defend herself if it caught her.

A fearsome bellow snapped her back into the moment.

She picked left. Sheriff Decker was in that direction, and he had the best tool ever, a loaded gun.

Chapter 66

WHAT WAS THAT?" Nancy asked. She reached out and held on to Decker's arm. "Why did the lights go out?"

"A transformer blowing. Probably took out power to half the town." Decker said.

"That's just great. How are we going to find Taylor now? I can't see two feet in front of me."

"The school has a backup generator. It should kick in any time now." As if on command, the overhead lights flickered and came back on, bathing the corridor in cool blue light.

"Oh, thank God," Nancy said.

"See, nothing to worry about." Decker motioned to Nancy. "Come on." They started down the corridor once more, moving at a quick pace. Outside, Decker could hear the storm, hear the rain drumming on the roof of the building, and the wind howling. Occasionally something bumped along overhead, a branch blown in the wind perhaps, or some other debris.

When they reached an intersection Nancy led them left. They rounded the corner, and there was Taylor. She was running toward them, her feet slapping the ground and echoing along the corridor. When she saw them a look of relief washed over her.

"There she is." Nancy took a step toward her daughter.

"Wait." Decker put his arm out, blocking Nancy's forward movement. "This isn't right."

"What are you doing?" Nancy shot him a confused glance. "What's wrong?"

Before he could reply Taylor answered for him. "It's behind me," she screamed, closing the distance between them and almost careening headlong into Decker.

"What is?" Nancy's eyes roamed the corridor.

"That." Decker pointed at a hulking shape that rounded the bend and appeared in the corridor behind the terrified teen.

"Oh, sweet mercy." Nancy recoiled in horror. "What is that thing?"

"Damned if I know." Decker pulled his gun and raised it.

"Don't let it get me." Taylor pleaded, placing the sheriff between herself and the approaching nightmare.

"It'll have to come through me first."

The beast slowed, slinking forward. It eyed Decker and the two women.

Decker motioned to Taylor and Nancy. "Get behind me." For a moment he hesitated, unable to tear his eyes from the nightmarish beast, but then his training snapped in. He aimed the gun and fired. The boom was deafening in the enclosed space.

The creature let out an enraged shriek, but kept coming.

"Run." Decker back peddled, keeping the gun aimed. "I'll hold it off here."

"Not a chance. I'm not leaving you here alone with that monster," Nancy said. "It will kill you."

"Not if I kill it first. Go. Get Taylor out of here." He racked the gun and squeezed off another shot. This one slammed into the beast's shoulder. The creature pivoted backward, almost knocked from its feet by the impact. Decker turned to Nancy, his face grim. "Move. Now."

"Alright, I'm going." Nancy took Taylor's hand and dragged her backward. It was useless to argue. Decker was right. She paused and looked back at him. "Don't die, please?"

"I'll do my best." Decker loaded another shot into the Glock's breach.

"I love you." She met his gaze, just for an instant, and then she turned and ran.

Decker planted himself firmly in the path of the approaching beast. If it reached the gymnasium, there would be a bloodbath, and he couldn't allow that to happen. He lifted the gun, aimed down the barrel, and squeezed the trigger.

Except the creature was not there anymore.

It was airborne, hurtling toward him with jaws wide and claws outstretched.

He fired twice in quick succession, missing each time. It was just too fast.

At the last second, as the creature made contact and sent him sprawling to the ground, Decker wished he'd told Nancy he loved her too. Because he couldn't tell her if he was dead. But it was too late now. He felt the beast's fetid breath on his face, a rotten stench that made him gag. He closed his eyes and waited to die.

The corridor erupted in a cacophony of ear-splitting sound. The creature flew up and back, releasing Decker. It let out a howl of pain.

Decker opened his eyes and sat up, grateful to be alive.

The beast lay sprawled on the tiles several feet away, blood seeping from a nasty wound below the right shoulder. It tried to rise, fought its way halfway up. A second blast rang out, knocking it back down to the floor.

Decker winced, ears ringing.

Someone walked past him brandishing a large-caliber hunting rifle. The newcomer walked right up to the prone beast, lowered the weapon, and fired again at point blank range. "That's for Terry."

Decker recognized the voice. Jeremiah Boudreaux. He dragged himself to his feet, expecting to see blood seeping through his shirt, but there was none. Through some miracle, he had escaped with bruises.

A hand landed on his shoulder. He looked around. Nancy was standing there, with Taylor behind her, a look of relief on her face.

Jeremiah walked toward them, the gun at his side, his face blank and emotionless.

"It's over," Nancy said, her voice loaded with relief.

Decker put his arm around her and held her close. He glanced back at Taylor. The girl still hovered behind them, unwilling to move any closer.

"Look out." Nancy's eyes flew wide.

Decker swiveled.

The beast wasn't dead. It shook its head, groggy, then rose to its feet.

It lurched forward.

"Move aside." Decker raised his gun.

Jeremiah, his back to the creature, looked startled.

Taylor screamed.

The creature sprang forward. It crashed into Jeremiah, pitching him forward. The gun flew from his grasp and landed, useless, several feet away. The beast let out a bellow of defiance and lashed out, opening a vicious wound across Jeremiah's back. The old man howled in pain.

Decker aimed his handgun. There were still ten rounds left, but the small firearm would not be powerful enough. He holstered it, eyeing the discarded rifle.

"Don't," Nancy gripped his arm. "It will kill you."

"I have too, or we're all dead."

He steadied his nerves and ran for the rifle, dropping like a baseball player sliding into fourth base, letting his momentum carry him forward.

The beast swatted, ripping the air above his head. Decker felt claws rake his skin, and then he was past.

The beast howled in frustration. It turned and snapped at him.

Decker scooped up the gun and raised it, pushing the barrel into the mouth of the creature as its jaws descended.

He pulled the trigger.

The beast's head erupted in a spray of blood and gore. It swayed for a moment, defying gravity, then toppled backward.

Decker scrambled up, gun at the ready, but this time the creature didn't move. It was dead.

He put a hand out and helped Jeremiah to his feet, then glanced back toward Nancy and Taylor to make sure they were safe.

When he looked back the creature was gone. In its place lay the naked, bloodied body of an old woman. The back of her head was missing, blown away by the rifle. Decker walked over to the corpse. He looked down. Annie Doucet's lifeless and bloodied face looked back up at him.

He turned to Nancy and dropped the gun. "It's over."

She paused a moment, then ran to him, throwing her arms around his neck. "You scared the hell out of me. Don't ever do that again."

"I'll do my best." Decker said. He glanced toward Jeremiah. "We should get that wound looked it."

"It's a scratch."

"It's a lot worse than that." Nancy took him by the arm. "Come on, let's all go back to the gym, and I'll patch you up."

"What about her?" Taylor nodded toward Annie Doucet. "We can't just leave her here. What if she's not dead?"

"She's dead," Decker replied. "Whatever she was, it can't hurt you now."

Chapter 67

DECKER SAT UP IN BED, his body dripping sweat. For the third time that week the nightmare had returned, the beast stalking him in the darkness, hunting him. Even now, as the dream faded, he could feel the weight of the creature as it pinned him to the ground, feel those wicked jaws as they tore into his flesh, slicing the jugular and cutting off his breath. He reached up and touched his neck, relived to find that everything was normal. There was no gaping wound, no blood. He looked at the glowing digits of the alarm clock next to the bed. 2:24 a.m. He'd barely gotten two hours of sleep before the nightmare woke him. Still, that was about an hour more than the last time.

"Did you have the dream again?" Nancy reached out, her voice soft and sleepy.

"Go back to sleep." Decker squeezed her hand. "I'm fine."

"You don't look fine. Maybe you should see a doctor. It might help if you talk to someone."

"I talk to you."

"I mean a professional."

"A shrink. What good is that? If I tell them what happened

they'll either put me in a straitjacket or take away my badge, maybe both."

"It does sound crazy," Nancy agreed. "Do you think we'll ever know what possessed Annie Doucet?"

"It's pretty obvious. She wanted to hurt the people that were hurting her, taking her land. The Mayor, members of the chamber like Benny Townsend and Jake's parents–" He took a breath. "She especially wanted to hurt you as Chamber president. The road was your idea. You championed the project. She figured you were taking the one thing she loved, so she would go after the thing you loved. Taylor."

"I get that. She wanted revenge. That's why she killed the moonshiner, Floyd. He sold his land to the town and took the money. She went after Ed too, because he was on the Chamber's board. He had a lucky escape."

"He did," Decker agreed. They had found Ed after the hurricane blew over, huddled in his wrecked car with a nasty lump on his noggin but otherwise okay.

Nancy nodded. "What I don't get is how? I mean, literally how she changed into a monster. What possessed her? What was that creature?"

"Beats me." Decker lay back and put his arm around her. "If you believe Ed Johnson, she was a Loup-Garou. A werewolf."

"And you?" Nancy looked at him. "Is that what you believe?"

"I believe what I saw in that school corridor." He shrugged. "It sure as hell wasn't a feeble old woman that killed the Mayor and almost killed us."

"Well, however she turned herself into that creature, she's gone and can't hurt anyone else ever again."

"You know what, I don't want to talk about this anymore." Decker pulled Nancy close.

"Me either." Nancy snuggled down next to Decker and placed her head on his chest.

"I love you, Sheriff John Decker," she said.

"I love you too," he replied. All was right with the world. There were no monsters lurking in the shadows, and for this moment, Decker was happy.

Epilogue

Three Months Later

JOHN DECKER EXITED the New Orleans courthouse and descended the steps to street level. For the last several hours he had been in a third-floor conference room fighting for his job. The inquiry into the events that took place in Wolf Haven's high school during the hurricane had dragged on for six weeks. During that period, Decker's reputation and integrity had been questioned. He had also spent a good portion of that time on paid suspension while his deputy took over the reins as interim town sheriff. By the time the final hearing rolled around, Decker was not sure that he even cared about the outcome. Annie Doucet's death had triggered a firestorm of media coverage and criticism that had left him frustrated and bitter. The court of public opinion had rendered their verdict and although there were some who believed Decker's version of events, they were in the minority. The six-member board of inquiry, with whom Decker had just spent a good portion of his day, were of the same opinion as a majority of the general public. They did not believe that Annie Doucet had run rampant in Wolf Haven on a killing spree that had culminated in the grisly death of Mayor Beau Thornton. In short, the idea that an elderly woman had transformed herself into a slathering beast in order to exact revenge upon those she felt had wronged her was a bridge too far. They had made it clear that the only reason he was not facing criminal charges was because the forensic evidence gathered at the scene of Mayor Thornton's demise backed Decker's claim that Annie Doucet was the killer. This hadn't stopped them from exacting their own brand of punishment, however. As of this very afternoon, Decker was no longer the Sheriff of Wolf Haven.

"Wait up." A voice called out over the din of Midtown traffic.

Decker turned to see Chad Hardwick racing down the steps, waving an arm. He felt a flash of anger. "What the hell do you want?"

"I thought we should clear the air." Chad came to a halt a few feet from Decker, breathing heavily. His sunglasses sat atop his head like a second pair of eyes.

"You could've cleared the air at any point over the last six weeks by telling the truth," Decker snapped. "We were supposed to have each other's backs. That's what good cops do."

"Look, I had nothing to do with what just went on in there. I'm sorry you lost your job, but if I'd backed you up and said that Annie Doucet turned herself into a wolf, we'd both be fired."

"You could at least have tried." Decker turned to walk away.

Chad reached a hand out and gripped Decker's arm. "This isn't how I want things to end."

"Are you kidding me?" Decker snatched his arm way. "You contradicted every statement I made to the board of inquiry. You twisted it to look like I was trying to cover something up with a crazy lie. You were more interested in saving your own hide than telling the truth."

"That hurts."

"I'm sure the promotion to sheriff will ease any minor pains you might be experiencing."

"Someone has to do the job." Chad shook his head. "Look, we both know what Annie Doucet was. But there's a difference between knowing something and speaking about it. You should've kept your mouth shut. Then maybe you would still be employed."

"And what kind of story do you think I could've conjured up that would have better explained shooting an old woman in a school corridor during a storm? A woman who, I might add, was buck naked at the time."

"Which was why I didn't back you up. The whole thing sounds crazy. There's no sane explanation that would satisfy that board of inquiry. You were always going to take the fall for this, but I was damned if I was going to let you drag me down too." Chad grinned and slid the sunglasses down over his eyes. "I'll see you back at the station. Yes?"

"What makes you think I'm going back there?"

"Because you have a desk to clear out, and I'd really like to move my stuff over before the weekend. Get a feel for the job, and all that."

"You're a snake, you know that?" Decker resisted the urge to rip the sunglasses from Chad's face, throw them on the ground, and stomp on them.

"I'm just taking advantage of a fortuitous situation." Chad's smile lifted into a smirk. "Oh, and Decker, don't drive too fast on the way back to town. Remember, you're a civilian now. I'd hate for you to get a speeding ticket." With those parting words, Chad strolled off toward his cruiser, which was waiting in a police-only bay in front of the courthouse.

"Asshole," Decker muttered under his breath and turned to walk in the other direction. His own car was parked four blocks away in a municipal lot.

He'd barely made it to the end of the street when his phone rang.

It was a number he didn't recognize with an out-of-state area code.

"Hello." He lifted the phone to his ear.

"Yes, hello. Is this Sheriff John Decker?" A female voice asked.

"This is John Decker. There's no need to address me as sheriff. That ship sailed this afternoon." Decker felt a pang of sadness at that. "What can I do for you?"

"My name is Haley Marsh. I'm the administrator for a small settlement in Alaska. Goes by the name of Shackleton."

"Never heard of it," Decker replied, wondering why a town official from Alaska was telephoning him.

"Few people have. We used to be a military base many moons ago but that's all changed. Like I said, it's a very small place. A speck on the map. Be that as it may, we have a rather large problem."

Decker stopped walking. "I'm sorry, I don't mean to be rude, but it's been a long and trying day. Would you mind getting to the point?"

"Absolutely. Of course. We wish to hire you."

"That's a very kind offer, Miss Marsh. Especially since I've only been unemployed for a little over fifteen minutes, but I don't want to move to Alaska."

"Heavens, we're not asking you to move here permanently." Haley laughed nervously. "We want to employ your services on a temporary basis. We've seen you on the news and you're exactly what we need."

"And what is it that you need?" Decker asked.

"A monster hunter, Mr. Decker. To stop the creature that's been killing our town folk." Haley drew in a sharp breath. "In short, we need you."

"A monster, huh?"

"So, will you come?"

"Call me in the morning, and we'll talk." Decker hung up the phone and pushed it back into his pocket. He started along the sidewalk once more. Today he would clean out his desk, go home to Nancy, and settle down with a bottle of Bourbon. Tomorrow he would probably agree to go to Alaska.

Made in the USA
Middletown, DE
31 May 2022

66461597R10130